FRUITS OF FALL LOVE

Amish Love Through the Seasons Book 3

Sylvia Price
Editor: Tandy O, Eagle Eye
Editing & Proofreading

Penn and Ink Writing, LLC

Copyright © 2021 Sylvia Price

All rights reserved

This is a work of fiction. Names, characters, places, and incidents are either products of the author's imagination or are used fictitiously. Any similarity to actual events or locales or persons, living or dead, is entirely coincidental.

No part of this publication may be reproduced, stored in or introduced into a retrieval system, or transmitted, in any form, or by any means (electronic, mechanical, photocopying, recording, or otherwise) without the prior written permission of the copyright owner. The author acknowledges the trademarked status and trademark owners of various products referenced status and trademark owners of various products referenced in this work of fiction, which have been used without permission. The publication/use of the trademarks is not authorized, associated with or sponsored by the trademark owners.

STAY UP-TO-DATE WITH SYLVIA PRICE

Subscribe to Sylvia's newsletter at newsletter.sylviaprice.com to get to know Sylvia and her family. It's also a great way to stay in the loop about new releases, freebies, promos, and more.

As a thank-you, you will receive a FREE exclusive short story that isn't available for purchase.

PRAISE FOR SYLVIA PRICE'S BOOKS

"Author Sylvia Price wrote a storyline that enthralled me. The characters are unique in their own way, which made it more interesting. I highly recommend reading this book. I'll be reading more of Author Sylvia Price's books."

"You can see the love of the main characters and the love that the author has for the main characters and her writing. This book is so wonderful. I cannot wait to read more from this beautiful writer."

"The storyline caught my attention from the very beginning and kept me interested throughout the entire book. I loved the chemistry between the characters."

"A wonderful, sweet and clean story with strong characters. Now I just need to know what happens next!"

"First time reading this author, and I'm very impressed! I love feeling the godliness of this story."

"This was a wonderful story that reminded me of a glorious God we have."

"I encourage all to read this uplifting story of faith and friendship."

"I love Sylvia's books because they are filled with love and faith."

OTHER BOOKS BY SYLVIA PRICE

Seeds of Spring Love (Amish Love Through the Seasons Book 1) – http://getbook.at/seedsofspring
Sprouts of Summer Love (Amish Love Through the Seasons Book 2) – http://getbook.at/sproutsofsummer
Fruits of Fall Love (Amish Love Through the Seasons Book 3) – http://getbook.at/fruitsoffall
Waiting for Winter Love (Amish Love Through the Seasons Book 4) – http://getbook.at/waitingforwinter

The Christmas Arrival – http://getbook.at/christmasarrival

Jonah's Redemption: Book 1 – FREE
Jonah's Redemption: Book 2 – http://getbook.at/jonah2
Jonah's Redemption: Book 3 – http://getbook.at/jonah3
Jonah's Redemption: Book 4 – http://getbook.at/jonah4
Jonah's Redemption: Book 5 – http://getbook.at/jonah5
Jonah's Redemption: Boxed Set – http://getbook.at/jonahset

Songbird Cottage Beginnings (Pleasant Bay Prequel) – FREE
The Songbird Cottage (Pleasant Bay Book 1) – http://getbook.at/songbirdcottage

Return to Songbird Cottage (Pleasant Bay Book 2) – http://getbook.at/returntosongbird
Escape to Songbird Cottage (Pleasant Bay Book 3) – http://getbook.at/escapetosongbird
Secrets of Songbird Cottage (Pleasant Bay Book 4) – http://getbook.at/secretsofsongbird
Seasons at Songbird Cottage (Pleasant Bay Book 5) – http://getbook.at/seasonsatsongbird
The Songbird Cottage Boxed Set (Pleasant Bay Complete Series Collection) – http://getbook.at/songbirdbox

CONTENTS

Title Page
Copyright
Stay Up-to-Date with Sylvia Price
Praise for Sylvia Price's Books
Other Books by Sylvia Price
Chapter 1: Changing Leaves — 1
Chapter 2: Serenity, Courage, and Wisdom — 8
Chapter 3: Home Industry — 18
Chapter 4: Back Home Again — 30
Chapter 5: Unexpected Visitors — 47
Chapter 6: I Have Light — 59
Chapter 7: Ashes — 68
Books In This Series — 77
Books By This Author — 79
About the Author — 85

CHAPTER 1: CHANGING LEAVES

"Cheer up," Aaron said to Mary, who stared unhappily at the garden. "It's not the end. We've just planted the root veggies, and they like the cold. Plus, we have some onions and garlic bulbs in the ground."

Mary appreciated Aaron's effort, but the garden just wasn't the same. In the spring and summer months, the garden had felt alive and had promised great yields with its bursts of color. Now that the yields were present, dull yellows and browns decorated the wilted leaves and vines. The warm air that had invited the youths outside had turned cold, pushing them all indoors. Of course, there were still some crops to harvest. The pumpkin patch was flourishing, and the apple trees stood burdened with fruit. There was work to be done, but the harvest would be terminal. After it, everything left behind would decay and die. Knowing that the end was near robbed the garden of its magic.

"*Danki* for coming today," Mary said.

"You're welcome," Aaron replied. "I'm sorry I can't stay as long as I'd like."

Mary was nevertheless grateful. Her smile told him so.

Times, though, had changed.

"Have any of the others been around?" Aaron asked.

Mary shook her head. Since the end of summer, the garden had seen fewer of its young tenders. Mary did not know it at the time, but the picnic Sarah Weaver and Jacob Beiler had enjoyed at the end of August had been the beginning of the end of the group's adventure. Ever since that day, they had struck out in pairs, seeking new adventures, mostly romantic ones, leaving Mary and Aaron with the bulk of the harvesting, weeding, and selling. By the end of August, they had all run out of excuses, so they simply ceased going.

"The summer is over," Abigael had pointed out, "and, with fall here, there is hardly anything to do. Besides, Aaron and Amos are both helping out on their farm with the harvests."

Though it wasn't true, Mary had not argued. The couples were now well established and were too busy planning their weddings and futures to care for a small community garden. Only Mary, Hannah, and Aaron continued to tend to the garden, although both Hannah and Aaron could not help as frequently as before. Abigael was right about Amos and Aaron. With Isaiah still in the hospital, they were expected to be at the farm to help with the harvest. Fall was a busy time in their community. Corn, tobacco, pumpkins, and soybeans were to be harvested, and, for the women, there were weddings to plan.

"Oh well, never mind," Aaron said cheerfully.

"How are the harvests going?" Mary asked.

Aaron shrugged. "As well as can be expected. Noah is doing a *gut* job, considering that it's his first harvest and that he's under a lot of pressure."

Mary nodded. She could imagine how difficult it must be

to coordinate such a thing. It was especially important for that farm's financial future.

"Well, I should get back." Aaron dusted the dirt off his pants and headed out.

Mary hid her disappointment. She did not want to make Aaron feel guilty for having to go so soon after he had arrived. After all, it was not his fault. Despite her best efforts, her eyes betrayed her. When Aaron noticed, he smiled sympathetically.

"Try not to be dispirited," Aaron said. "I know that things have changed, but perhaps it's best to move on from how things were and to embrace how things are now. After all, every season is glorious in its own way."

Mary inhaled and turned to look at the garden. It held no beauty. Only chores. Though Aaron could provide new perspectives on things, he was unable to show Mary what he saw. She sighed.

"I promise I'll try not to feel too sad that summer is gone," Mary said.

Aaron nodded and left.

Mary retreated to her favorite spot under the dogwood tree. The leaves, which had been a brilliant shade of green only a fortnight ago, were now changing to a pale shade of red. In another week, it would look as though it were on fire. *Such memories under this tree!* she thought, recalling balmy afternoons spent outstretched on the grass eating cold pork sandwiches. The wind whispered to the leaves, gently presaging a storm or a change of season. Other times, the gang had retreated beneath its limbs in the rain, as chicks to a hen. Beneath that canopy had been a happy place filled with laughter, gossip, and youth. How bittersweet were the memories to Mary, presently. She clutched her heart to dull its longing and comfort its loneliness.

Mary's morning in the garden with Aaron had temporarily relieved her anxiety. His laughter and wit had brightened her gloom. Spending time with Aaron had felt like old times. (Oh! the irony of youth, reminiscing of blossoms when they are, as yet, unripe!) Though she missed all her friends, Aaron was missed the most.

The trouble with having spent so much time alone of late was that Mary found herself trapped in her own thoughts. For Mary, her head could be a scary place when confronted with all her suppressed feelings, especially the ones about Aaron. Mary had a difficult time knowing how she felt about him, though she was too immature to realize that feelings aren't sorted in the brain. Abigael and Sarah, on the other hand, seemed certain about their men. They had known exactly how they felt, with minimal angst. However, no matter how hard Mary tried, her heart was torn.

Spring and summer had so preoccupied Mary with the garden, the roadside stand, and the markets, that she had ignored her sorrow over being without a partner. However, Fast Day and its formal announcements of the upcoming marriages was only a few days away. That revelation had made Mary feel left out. She could picture her father reading out the names of the girls who were to be married, mostly her classmates. After that, the fathers would then announce the dates and times of the weddings, and they'd invite everyone in the congregation to attend. Noah would stand in Isaiah's stead to announce Amos. The Weaver twins, Amos, and Jacob would not be in church when announced, accentuating the loneliness.

Granted, Mary was happy for them all. Nevertheless, she

also feared she may have been too single-minded in trying to help the Fishers, and that, as a result, the garden had taken over. Its end was now galloping toward her, leaving her destitute of friends. For, all through December, January, and February, the married girls would travel to visit relatives on a honeymoon tour to collect gifts. The winter had not yet come upon her, yet it made her shiver.

Mary's current predicament was exacerbated by her indecision toward Aaron. She simply could not come to a conclusion about her feelings for him. Any hope that Aaron would make the first move was nullified by his good ole friendly self. *Rachel might have the answers,* she thought. So, she set off to find her.

"How did you know that Noah was the one for you?" Mary asked her older sister. "Did you just know all at once, or was it gradual?"

Rachel looked surprised because it was unusual for her sister to ask questions about romance. "Well, you know it was complicated for Noah and me because of Samuel." She cleared her throat. "But I knew I was attracted to Noah the moment I saw him. I tried to deny it until I learned that those kinds of feelings can't just be wished away."

Mary sighed. Rachel was exactly like Abigael and Sarah, who had found love simply by looking. Truth be told, however, it was Mary who had insisted that an unspeakable feeling in the pit of a girl's stomach was evidence of love, when discussing the matter with her sister when they had still shared a bedroom. In fact, she had chided her for not feeling thus with her then fiancé, Sam. The junior Lapp was now trying to convince herself that she'd outgrown her childish convictions about love. Indeed, she had anticipated a fluttering in her tummy when she had beheld Aaron, yet none had come. *Surely,* she thought, *it must be because there is no truth to such things. They are mere assumptions. There must be something cerebral involved in falling in love.* Aaron was a handsome boy, but she did not know if that meant she was attracted to him. Logically, she ought to be. "But how do you *know* when you are attracted to someone?"

"It's more of a feeling. I suppose it's what they refer to as chemistry. You can't really explain it but it's just there. Does that answer your question?"

To Mary, Rachel's answer was as clear as mud, but it covered everything.

"Try not to overthink it. Often, love finds us."

Mary held her breath. It was easy for Rachel to spout such wisdom. After all, she had already found the man she loved and who loved her. She, on the other hand, was doomed to live a life alone unless she figured out what she wanted. Perhaps seeing him again might provoke some "chemistry." Mary set off to find Aaron.

As fate would have it, there was neither sight nor sound of Aaron. He was not in the barn, nor in any of the usual fields. She wondered over to the neighbors to see if they'd seen him.

Mrs. Yoder stood in the vegetable garden at the side of her house, harvesting tomatoes.

"Hello, Mrs. Yoder," greeted Mary.

"Oh hello, Mary," Mrs. Yoder replied in surprise.

"Have you seen Aaron?" Mary asked.

"Noah has the boys out in the east field," Mrs. Yoder explained. "But he won't thank you for going and disturbing Aaron. They are on a tight schedule."

Mary nodded, trying not to look too disappointed, but her

bottom lip stuck out, giving her away.

"I'll tell him you're looking for him," Mrs. Yoder offered.

"Oh no, don't worry. It wasn't anything important. I just thought that if he were around, I'd say hello."

Mrs. Yoder smiled wryly but said nothing.

"*Danki*, Mrs. Yoder. See you around."

Mary hurried back down toward the main road. She was finding it increasingly difficult to stick to her plan, especially as Aaron was never around. From the Fishers', Mary headed straight to the garden. It had been a few days since they had planted the root vegetables, and Mary wished to water the beds and ensure that everything was in order. As she walked down the narrow paths, leaves crunched softly beneath her boots, the willows and ash trees having shed most of their leaves. Other trees, though, still clung tightly to their dying foliage, unwilling to let go of summer. Mary sighed and pulled her shawl around her shoulders. There was a distinct chill in the air for which Mary was not ready. Fall had seemed to come out of nowhere, and with it, the end of something for which Mary greatly cared: her garden.

Preoccupation with thoughts of Aaron had prevented Mary from noticing a figure standing under the dogwood tree. Once she noticed, she assumed it was Hannah. But, as she got closer, it was clearly not one of the young gardeners. She was a stranger.

CHAPTER 2: SERENITY, COURAGE, AND WISDOM

A woman stared up at the dogwood tree, captivated by its fiercely red leaves. Unused to strangers, Mary was captivated by the outsider. Unwilling to disturb such a moment, the bishop's daughter was content to observe the woman staring at the tree from a distance. Surely the visitor was unaware that she was being watched.

"It's a beautiful tree," the woman said, startling Mary. "They say that dogwoods spend the entire summer absorbing the rays from the sun so that, when fall comes, they can radiate light and beauty onto the dying earth."

Such prose intrigued the youth. The Amish in Erie spoke in plainer language. She leaned forward, wishing to know more about this woman.

"I'm sorry. I didn't mean to trespass. I was walking along, and I saw the dogwood from the road, and I couldn't help myself." The woman turned and smiled, but Mary was put off by her swollen belly.

"It's you," Mary said without thinking, "the newcomer."

The woman continued to smile as she nodded.

Finally hearing what she had said, Mary raised her hand to her mouth. "I'm sorry. That was thoughtless of me."

"Don't fret," the woman said as she placed her right hand on her stomach. "I'm the intruder here in your garden." Sadness lurked beneath her smile.

News that a pregnant widow had moved to the community had spread soon after her arrival, yet no one had seen much of the woman, nor did anyone know her story. She was a mystery to their community.

"You're not an intruder," Mary said. "Anyone is welcome here in the garden."

"Well, that is *gut* news because I think it's quite lovely, and I fear that my heart would break should I be sent away and told never to return."

Mary smiled. She sensed that they might be kindred spirits. "My name is Mary Lapp."

The woman's eyes widened. Mary guessed it was because she was the bishop's daughter. "It's nice to meet you, Mary. My name is Adel."

Now, Mary's eyes widened. Such a name had never been heard in her community. It was pretty and mysterious, much like the woman herself. "I hope you don't think it's rude of me to say that you have an unusual name."

Adel chuckled. "You're right, Mary. It is not a common *Amisch* name. My *groosseldre* (grandparents) were from Switzerland, and they moved to America. My *maem* named me Adel after my *urgroossmudder* (great grandmother)."

"It's a lovely name. I wish I had such an interesting name. What does it mean?"

"Noble," Adel answered.

"It suits you."

"And Mary suits you."

Mary wrinkled her nose.

Adel smiled. "Mary is a very beautiful name, albeit a traditional one. Do you know what it means?"

Mary shook her head.

"It means 'beloved.'"

Mary wished she had found out sooner.

"If it's not an inconvenience, may I come and work in your garden?"

Mary was taken aback, and her face betrayed her, for Adel suddenly looked uncomfortable.

"I'm sorry. It was presumptuous of me to ask such a thing. After all, I'm new to the community, and you don't know me."

"It's not that. You just took me by surprise. You are most welcome to come and work in the garden."

"*Danki* Mary," Adel said. Her smile returned.

"Would you like me to show you around?" Mary asked.

Adel hesitated. "I would very much like that, Mary, but I'm afraid that I have an appointment in town, and I'm already late. How about I meet you here tomorrow?"

"*Ya*," Mary agreed.

"Same time?"

Mary nodded enthusiastically.

"Goodbye, Mary. It was lovely to meet you."

"You, too."

Mary stood and watched the pretty woman leave the garden and disappear over the hill. What had transpired was unusual, yet the unusual was necessary for Mary to feel the magic of the garden again. She hurried off to visit her sister.

"Have you met the newcomer?" Mary asked once seated in Rachel's kitchen.

Rachel shook her head. "No, I had heard that she moved here from a community out West, but she has been keeping to herself, it seems."

"I met her."

Rachel turned to her younger sister with great interest. "You did? When?"

"Just before I came here. She was in the garden."

"Really? How odd. What did she say?"

"She told me that her name is Adel, and she wants to come and work in the garden."

Rachel frowned. "What did you tell her?"

"I said she was welcome to work in the garden."

Rachel's brows knitted together.

"What?" Mary asked.

"Nothing. Well, it's just we don't know this woman or her story. Do you think it's prudent?"

Mary shrugged. "Well, she's Amish. She seemed nice enough to me."

Rachel paused. "You're right, Mary. Who am I to judge her, after all?"

"So, tell me, how is Isaiah?" Mary asked, changing the subject.

Rachel explained Isaiah's progress over the last few weeks, how he was doing so well and that he might come home soon. As Mary listened, she was distracted by her impending rendezvous with Adel in the garden the following day. She was looking forward to showing her all the work done, telling her Isaiah's story, and getting to know her.

The next day, Mary waited underneath the dogwood trees for Adel. She had already planned it all out in her head—she would show her the newly planted crops first and then take her around to see the other beds. The small garden gate squeaked, and Adel came walking toward her wearing a friendly smile.

"Hello, Mary. It's lovely to see you again."

"And you," Mary agreed. "Are you ready to see the garden?"

Adel nodded, still smiling like a child who'd made a new friend.

"This way," Mary said. She led Adel around the garden, chatting away about all that was planted and what had been harvested.

"The pumpkins are ready to harvest."

Adel listened quietly. They walked around the garden for half an hour before Mary remembered that her guest was pregnant. "Perhaps you'd like to rest? There is a bench just ahead."

Adel nodded. They headed toward the small, stone bench at the edge of the garden near the Weaver home.

"You've done a wonderful job here, Mary."

"I didn't do it alone," Mary explained. "I had a lot of help."

"Where are the other gardeners?"

Mary shrugged and looked out across the garden. "There isn't anyone left but me. Aaron and Hannah come sometimes, but the others are all coupled together and planning their weddings. They don't have time for the garden anymore."

"I can understand your disappointment," Adel said, "but I'm also happy for your friends. Sometimes, love can be a powerful, all-consuming force. When love is found, everything else seems to pale in comparison."

Adel's homesickness was apparent. She yearned for something, something she missed. *But why doesn't she go back?* Mary thought. Alas! Youth are seldom able to recognize when someone is speaking from the other side of love.

"May I ask why you came to Pennsylvania?"

"I'm not sure you wish to know," Adel replied.

"I do wish to know if you want to tell me."

Adel sighed, then placed her palm against her tummy. "It is not a happy story, Mary, although it began as the happiest story of all. Daniel and I loved each other from the moment we learned what love was. At first, we were just children, the best of friends. Yet friendship is how all great love starts. Trust, acceptance, and support set the strongest foundation for any relationship. As we grew older, our friendship blossomed. It turned into something for which neither of us could have prepared. Daniel and I realized that we were completely and utterly preoccupied with one another. When our time came, we were married. But it was not without its challenges. Daniel's parents had hoped he might marry another, and while they did not dispute our union, it was clear to me that they were not wholly happy with us either. Still, it did not matter, for we had each other, and the future lay before us, full of possibilities. The first year of our marriage was perfect except for one thing. Daniel and I both longed for a family of our own, yet after a year of trying, we had no luck." Adel paused and gently moved her hand over her stomach.

"I wanted to get a professional opinion, but Daniel and his family were more traditional. He kept telling me that if *Gott* wanted us to have *kinner*, then He would make it happen. I tried to have faith. Every night I would go to bed, and I would pray for *Gott* to give us *kinner*. Still, the months passed, and nothing happened. I was resentful. I could not understand how we could be refused such a privilege. It burned me to witness all my classmates having *bobblin*; it was unbearable.

"A week before our second wedding anniversary, we found out that we were going to have a *bobbli*, and it was one of the happiest days of our lives. The news even brought Daniel's parents and me closer. It seemed as if everything had fallen into place." Tears welled up in her eyes. Mary inhaled, her first breath since Adel had begun. "Little did I know that everything would unravel."

Mary waited. Tears synchronously ran down their cheeks.

"I'm sorry," Mary said. "I shouldn't have asked."

Adele shook her head. "No, it's okay. It feels *gut* to be able to tell someone."

Mary looked down at her hands laying helplessly on her lap.

"It was an accident," Adel whispered. "It was late and raining heavily. Daniel had been on his way back from town. A driver lost control of his truck. There wasn't anything that anyone could have done. My Daniel was gone."

Mary felt a knot in her throat. "I'm so sorry," she whispered.

Adel nodded, then wiped the tears from her eyes. "After Daniel's death, I felt lost. It was only our *bobbli* that kept me tethered. My in-laws insisted that I move in as I had no family of my own. It seemed the logical choice, but I knew in my heart I could not do that. I knew that I needed to find a place where I could raise this *bobbli* without the heaviness of my grief and devastation. I thought that if I moved away, perhaps I could leave the painful memories behind me."

"Did it work?" Mary asked.

Adel smiled sadly. "No," she admitted. "But I believe that moving away was the right decision for me and my *bobbli*. While not everyone may agree with my decision to raise this *bobbli* alone, it's what I needed to do to move on."

Mary thought that Adel was the bravest person that she had ever met, and she wished she would have said that instead of what she said next. "I don't know much about death, but I've seen it in my garden. I've seen the flowers withering and dying and the vegetables busy rotting in their beds." She shut up as soon as she heard what she'd said. Unsure of what to do next and growing ever more anxious at the awkward silence—plus, her comfort at being silent now withered, thus causing more anxiety—Mary apologized: "I am sorry. That was insensitive."

"It's okay," Adel said. "Your garden has given you an experience of death. You will learn that ends are but the start of a new beginning. For the end of life will always give rise to new life."

"I just wish it were easy to let things go," Mary lamented.

"So do I. But if Daniel's death has taught me anything, it is to try to let go of the things that I cannot change."

Mary nodded and looked across the garden. A flock of white-throated sparrows was seated on the fence near the gate. Mary knew that they were preparing for their long journey south. She then closed her eyes.

God, give me the grace to accept with serenity the things that cannot be changed, courage to change the things which should be changed, and the wisdom to distinguish the one from the other.

In the ensuing days, Mary did not share Adel's story with anyone else. After all, it was not her story to tell. She felt privileged that Adel had chosen to tell her. Adel and Mary often met to work together in the garden. Mary was amazed by Adel's gardening abilities. The former became the latter's disciple and seemed to be learning something new from her every day.

"What inspired you to start this garden?" Adel asked one day. "Have you always been a gardener?"

It suddenly dawned on Mary that, while Adel had revealed her story, Mary had not shown her the same courtesy. "No," Mary admitted. "I never had much interest in gardening. But last winter, my sister's husband's uncle was hit by a truck and almost died." She paused, sensitive that the facts would remind Adel of her tragedy. "He's Aaron's father. He has three boys. Their mother died a while ago. So…" Mary's voice trailed off, hoping Adel was savvy enough to connect the dots.

"So, what happened?" Adel asked, softly.

"They managed to get him to the hospital in time, and he was okay, but he's had some major setbacks over the last few months."

"How long has he been in the hospital? Adel asked.

"The accident was at the end of February. So, seven months."

Adel shook her head. "That's awful. How is his family doing?"

"They have struggled. It's been difficult for everyone. One of the hardest parts has been the hospital bills."

Adel nodded. She knew that the Amish had no medical insurance.

"So, that's why I started the garden. I wanted to help pay some of the hospital bills."

"That's very admirable of you, Mary. I'm happy to hear that you are taking care of your own at such a young age. You should be proud."

Mary looked downcast.

"What's wrong?" Adel asked,

"It was going so well," Mary lamented, "but now I fear that

after the harvest we won't have a way to keep helping Isaiah."

"Try not to worry. I'm sure that we can think of something."

Mary nodded more from the weight of dead ideas collected at the front of her mind than as a sign of agreement. Still, she had heard, "...we can think of something." Adel may be just whom she needed.

And, indeed, she was. A week after they had first met in the garden, Mary and Adel were walking home when Adel stopped.

"What is it?" Mary asked, concerned for her pregnant friend.

"I have an idea about how we can help Mr. Fisher."

Mary was curious.

"I'll figure out the finer details, and then I'll share the plan with you."

Mary wondered what Adel might be planning but thought it wise to wait. New anxieties would only compound the old ones. Adel was a new friend. Though inspired by the woman several years her senior, Mary remained cautious. In many ways, Adel reminded her of Rachel. Both women were strong but vulnerable, and they both processed the world in a more systematic way. They were cerebral. Mary would just have to be patient.

"Simply know that there is hope," assured Adel.

CHAPTER 3: HOME INDUSTRY

Another week passed before Adel was ready to divulge her plan for the garden to help Isaiah Fisher. She had been tight-lipped about what her plan entailed. Mary brought it up only once. Adel told her that she was not ready to reveal her idea yet, a response that made the girl shy to ask again. Nevertheless, she remained desperate to know. Brooding in her frustrated curiosity at the garden gate, she was surprised by Adel, whom she had not noticed approaching.

"Will you tell me now?" Mary asked, speaking before thinking.

Adel had not been expecting the ambush, and her eyes widened. She understood exactly for what Mary was asking.

"Please," Mary begged, "I don't think I can go another moment without knowing."

Adel chuckled. "All right. I'm sorry to keep you waiting. But let's go and sit down, first."

The pair made their way through the garden to the stone bench. Mary listened intently.

"Ever since you told me about Mr. Fisher, I have been trying to think of a way we might help him further," Adel began. "I think that you have been doing very well with your roadside stand. But looking around at all of the food that is ready to harvest, I fear that we have too much to sell."

"I agree," said Mary. It had become apparent that there was no buggy large enough to contain what they had for sale and no community near that was large enough to absorb the harvest. The garden had produced a mighty yield, and Mary could not bear such waste.

"So, I was trying to think of a solution to this problem, and I think I have found it." Adel paused, enjoying Mary's undivided attention.

Mary seemed ready to jump out of her seat. She could not bear a cliffhanger, not now.

"All week, I have been doing research and gathering everything that we will need, and I finally think that we are ready." Adel paused again.

The suspense was too much for Mary. "Please tell me!"

Adel smiled. "I think that we must harvest all of the fruit and vegetables and we repurpose those we cannot sell. We will create an assortment of homemade foods such as jams, marmalades, pies, and casseroles. That way, we can sell things months after the fresh produce has been harvested, and for a higher price. Nothing will go to waste." She smiled, proud of herself. It had been a while since another had hung on to her every word. She missed it.

It was such an ingenious idea that Mary was sorry she had not thought of it first.

"So, what do you think?" Adel asked.

"I think it's *wunderbaar*!" Mary exclaimed.

Adel looked pleased. "*Gut*, then it's settled."

"What do we do first?" Mary asked.

"I think that we should harvest all of the fruits and vegetables that are ready, and anything that is not fit to sell fresh needs be repurposed at once."

"Okay," Mary agreed. "My only concern is that there is much harvesting to be done, and you're not supposed to be doing such heavy work."

"Don't worry about me," Adel assured her. "I'm tougher than you think."

Mary was skeptical. Adel risked much in doing heavy lifting, particularly since she carried Daniel's only possible offspring. Some of those pumpkins weighed a ton. "I will ask Aaron and Hannah if they might be able to help us."

"That would be *gut*," Adel agreed.

Thus, the harvest was put off until Mary could recruit the help of her friends. Mary hoped that Aaron and Hannah would not let her down. She said goodbye to Adel and then headed for the Fisher farm.

Evidence of the harvest season could be seen on both sides of the dirt road. Every field boasted farmhands working tirelessly in preparation for the barren months ahead. All the hay stood baled, and the air smelled sweet from the Kings' peach and apple orchards, which were a beehive of activity. Everyone moved with purpose and energy. Men in straw hats with baskets busily picked the juicy fruit. The trees breathed a sigh of relief as their branches were freed of the yoke of their great bounty.

Harvest time in their community was always a time of hard work. The men would work out in the fields while the women worked in the kitchen. Their community did not use modern practices as the English did, and so everything was done by hand. Harvest time was hard work, but it also brought the whole community together as they prepared for winter, and that was a beautiful thing.

Mary hoped that Hannah would not mind her showing up unannounced. She climbed the porch steps and knocked on the screen door. Mrs. King opened the door.

"Good afternoon Mrs. King. Is Hannah home?"

"She is," Mrs. King said. "Hannah?"

Light footsteps announced Hannah before she appeared. "Mary! What a nice surprise."

"It's good to see you, too," Mary said. "I was wondering if you might be able to come and help with the harvest in the garden tomorrow."

Hannah looked stern, the face she normally made before she disappointed someone with her answer. "I wish I could, Mary, but my *Mammi* is coming tomorrow. I am to cook the apples and the peaches for jam. I don't think *Maem* would allow me to help with the garden."

Mary nodded. The Amish harvest was the busiest time of year. Rest came in the winter. Still, Mary knew that she had to try.

"I understand."

"I'm sorry."

"Well, I'd better be going." Mary offered a paltry wave. Hannah had been her best hope.

"I hope to see you soon."

Mary regained the road, turned left, and headed for the Fisher farm. She could not help but feel rejected before she had made her request. A man during harvest was not easily spared.

"Hello, Mary," Noah said. "What can I do for you?"

Mary smiled as she approached him, but Noah did not look up from his task.

"Is Aaron around?"

"He's in the east field with some of the others."

"May I go and speak to him?"

"Sure," Noah agreed.

Mary thanked him and headed toward the east field. The farmhands were all hard at work. Aaron was at some distance with his back to her. It became apparent to Mary, as she approached, that he was hot and exhausted. Guilt almost choked her request for help in the garden.

"Hello," Aaron said in surprise.

"Hi," Mary responded.

Aaron's face was wet with perspiration, and in his hands were a bunch of corn stalks. "I didn't expect to see you today." He did not stop working as he spoke. He gathered the pile of corn stalks at his feet and carried them across to the large compost pile. Mary followed behind him, picking up the stalks that he dropped.

"I didn't expect to come today."

"What can I do for you?" Aaron asked.

"Well, I hate to ask, but is there any chance you might be able to help me in the garden tomorrow. We want to harvest the crops that are ready."

Aaron grimaced.

"It's fine if you can't," Mary blurted. "I can see you have a lot to do."

Aaron sighed. "I can't make you any promises, Mary, but I shall do my best to make time to help you tomorrow."

"*Danki*," Mary said. "I won't keep you any longer from your work. Goodbye." Mary turned to leave.

"How are you?" Aaron asked.

Mary turned back to him. There was a softness in his eyes.

"I'm fine," Mary answered.

"I'm happy to hear that. I've missed seeing you these last couple of weeks."

"I've missed you, too," Mary managed without blushing.

One of the farmhands called out to Aaron from across the field. "I'd better go," he said. "Hopefully, I'll see you tomorrow."

"Hopefully," Mary agreed.

Mary met Adel at the garden the following day.

"Is anyone else coming?" Adel asked.

"Aaron said he would try."

"Well, we shall just do the very best we can without them," Adel asserted.

Mary and Adel harvested the apples and peaches, carefully placing the fruit in the palms of their hands and twisting gently to lift the fruit slightly and pull it off the tree. It was a new experience for Mary, but Adel had harvested fruit before. She seemed a master at the technique.

"You see where the indentation is at the top of the apple?" Adel asked. "You know an apple is ready to be picked when it changes from green to yellow. You will notice that fruit which is ready to be harvested will come away from the branch without difficulty."

"As it is ready to be picked," Mary noted.

"Precisely. Nature is amazing."

They worked quickly for the first hour, then Adel strained to maintain her pace.

"Why don't you take a break?" Mary insisted.

"I'm fine," Adel said. She did not want to be babied. Such is the habit of first-time mothers; they think they can do everything they did before being with child. Another pregnancy or two would cure Adel of her delusion. Presently, however, Mary had to contend with her ambition. As she was about to argue with her new friend, Mary was interrupted by the sound of approaching hooves. It was Aaron arriving with the cart.

"Did someone request a healthy, young farmhand?" Aaron asked, smiling broadly.

Mary beamed. "Adel, this is Aaron Fisher."

Adel smiled warmly at Aaron. He bowed his head, respectfully.

"*Danki*, for coming to help us," Adel said.

"It's my pleasure," Aaron replied. "Noah gave me the afternoon to help you. I thought we could load up everything onto the cart so that it's ready for the roadside stand on Saturday."

"Actually," Mary looked sideways to her friend, "could we possibly take the cart to

Adel's house?"

"Huh?" Aaron said.

Mary explained the plan. Aaron was impressed. He looked solemnly grateful at the widow. "I think it's an excellent idea. My *daed* will be most grateful to you, as will I."

Adel was pleased.

"Well, we should get back to work," Mary said.

For the remainder of the afternoon, the trio worked tirelessly to harvest all the ripe

fruit and vegetables. Mary worried about Adel, but, as with most Amish women, the latter was unafraid of hard work, no matter her condition. Mary made sure she kept hydrated, her mothering instinct amusing Adel to no end.

By the time they finished work, the Fisher cart was loaded with a variety of fresh produce. There were apples, peaches, lemons, pumpkins, cranberries, winter squash, and a variety of greens.

"Just think of all of the wonderful things we can make," Mary exclaimed.

"This is an impressive harvest," Aaron agreed.

Mary and Adel climbed onto the cart beside Aaron and set off for Adel's house, a smallholding on the edge of town. Once there, they unloaded the produce into Adel's pantry and all over her floor. When they were done, there was no room to move.

"We had better get to work quickly," Adel said. "There is much to be done."

"Should I come around first thing tomorrow?" Mary asked.

"*Ya.*"

"Very well, I'll see you after breakfast."

Mary and Aaron said their goodbyes and climbed aboard the cart.

"*Danki,* Aaron," Mary said, "for coming to help today."

"I'm glad I came. It was nice to get away from the farm for a few hours, and truth be told, I missed the garden. I appreciate what you've done for our family."

"It was *gut* having you. It felt like old times."

Aaron nodded. Mary was too exhausted to hold any kind of conversation. Aaron did not pry. Thus, they were content to be in each other's company.

Upon a good night's sleep, Mary wolfed down her breakfast. Her parents stared. Mary got up from the table and headed for the door.

"Where are you off to in such a hurry?" Mrs. Lapp asked. "Surely not the garden, so early?"

Mary shook her head, not wanting to talk with her mouth full. "No," she said after swallowing. "I am going to Adel's house to begin repurposing the excess fruit and vegetables from the harvest."

Mrs. Lapp frowned but held her peace. Mary knew how people in the community felt about Adel. She also knew that the Amish prized uniformity of thought and deed, so she could easily predict her mother's attitude. It would be the same as the rest. While they all had the best intentions not to judge the young widow, it was strange (to the Erie community) that she had abandoned her friends and family to move to another community to raise her baby, alone. Mary was, in all likelihood, the only one to whom Adel had explained why she had made such a choice.

"Well, make sure you aren't late for supper," Mrs Lapp advised. "We may not be a farming family, but that doesn't mean there aren't things that need doing around here, too."

"*Ya, Maem,*" Mary said heading out of the door.

Adel's home smelled of sweet, roasted apples. Adel opened the door to greet Mary with the warm aroma of cinnamon and nutmeg. Mary's heart sang.

"I hope you don't mind that I got started already," Adel said. "I was up with the sparrows this morning. Everyone always talks about how you don't sleep when the baby arrives, but hardly anyone mentions pregnancy insomnia."

Mary gave Adel a sympathetic look. "My *schweschder*, Rachel, also struggled with insomnia when she was pregnant. She used to take six teaspoons of tart cherry juice every day."

"Perhaps I'll try that. Oh! how rude of me. Please come in."

Mary smiled before stepping into the house. The pair headed straight for the kitchen.

"I've just put the final tray of apples in the oven to bake," Adel said. "Once they are done, I thought we could make a batch of applesauce and apple butter. And then, if there is anything left over, we could make apple pie."

"That sounds *wunderbaar*."

"I went to see Mr. Troyer at the general store," Adel said. "I told him what we were doing, and he managed to give me an extra box of Mason jars. But can you keep a secret? I promised not to tell any of the other women folk."

Mary understood why Mr. Troyer had made that request. Mason jars were in high demand during harvest time for jams, marmalades, and pickled foods.

"Shall we get to work, then?" Adel suggested.

Mary nodded. She pulled her apron out from her basket and tied it about her waist. "Let's get cooking!"

Adel grinned, and together, they began to work on their array of homemade treats. The apples transformed into pies and the peaches into cobbler. The stress and worry that Mary had been suffering since the turn of the season dissolved into the butter and sugar. The arrival of fall and the harvest had meant the end of the garden and her work to help Isaiah. Yet, Adel had shown her that fall was merely the beginning of something new. They both worked until lunch.

"How about we sample some of our labors?" Adel suggested.

"*Ya*," Mary agreed. "After all, it would be irresponsible to sell products that have not been tested first."

Adel smiled her agreement. She reached for a fresh loaf of

bread, sliced it, and placed it onto a tray. "Pass me a jar of the apple butter and the peach jam."

Mary did as she was asked. Adel placed them on the tray beside the bread.

"I think that I have some cold pork in the pantry. Do you want to pour some tea in the meantime?"

Mary nodded. The women inspected their feast before eating it.

"Well, that looks like quite a spread," Adel said.

Mary admired the tray loaded with food.

"There is a small table in the back garden." How about we dine *alfresco*?"

Mary agreed and picked up the heavy tray. Together, they went outside and into the yard. It was a glorious autumn afternoon.

"The weather this fall has been some of the best I've ever experienced," Adel said.

"Autumn in Pennsylvania is *wunderbaar*," Mary agreed. "It's the winters you need to look out for."

"*Ya*. I've been warned about the winters around here."

Mary looked at Adel curiously.

"Some of the folk in my old community," Adel explained. "When they heard I was leaving, they tried to warn me off moving here. Their main tactic of dissuasion was the winter weather."

"Well, they are not wrong," Mary said.

"I hope the *bobbli* comes before the first snow," Adel said.

"When do you expect the *bobbli*?" Mary asked.

"I'm not entirely sure. I suspect there are around six or seven weeks left."

Mary nodded and glanced at Adel's bulging belly. Amish

women did not always have a due date like the English women. They knew that the baby would come in God's good timing and in His way.

"Are you afraid?" Mary asked.

Adel did not answer immediately. "A little. I'm not afraid of giving birth. I know that *Gott* will be watching over me, but I am afraid of doing it on my own."

"You do not need to do it on your own," Mary said. "I'll be there if you want me to."

Adel smiled warmly. "That's very kind of you, Mary. And a great comfort."

"Have you found a birthing *maem*?"

Adel looked at her in surprise.

"My *schweschder* had a *bobbli*, remember? I am well versed in births."

Adel chuckled. "After just one? Well, I suppose at least one of us is prepared."

"You must find one," Mary insisted.

Adel nodded. She had planned to find a birthing mother as soon as she arrived in Erie, but the garden and Mary had been a welcome distraction. Adel had also been hesitant to find a new birthing mother as she did not know any of the women in the community well enough to trust them with her beloved Daniel's only child. Perhaps Mary's sister could recommend someone. It would be wise, indeed, should the baby come before she expected it. "I will, Mary, I promise. Thank you for your concern."

Mary looked satisfied. She could finally enjoy their bread and preserves.

CHAPTER 4: BACK HOME AGAIN

Mary sat on the wooden floor in the Fishers' living room. She was busy helping Thomas make a 'Welcome Home' banner for Isaiah. It had been three days since word had come from the doctors that Isaiah could come home. Since then, the Fisher household had been a hub of excitement.

"I'm going to hang this banner right across the door!" Thomas declared.

"Perhaps you should hang it over the door," Mary suggested.

Thomas looked puzzled. "Why?"

"Because if you hang it across the door, how will anyone get in and out of the house?" Mary asked.

"I don't want anyone to get out of the house," Thomas said finally. "I'm tired of people leaving. I want everyone to stay together forever."

Mary smiled sympathetically. The little boy had been brave and patient while his father was in the hospital. "You know what, Tommy? I think that this banner is so *wunderbaar* that everyone deserves to see it. So why don't we hang it on the front gate for everyone who drives past?"

"*Ya!*" Thomas yelled in excitement.

Rachel stepped into the room. Thomas jumped up.

"Rachel, Mary said I could hang my banner outside of the gate so the whole town can see it."

"I think that's a lovely idea," Rachel agreed. "Aaron and Amos are outside, fixing the porch swing. Why don't you go out and ask them to help you once they're done?"

Thomas nodded and hurried out of the room.

Mary got up from the floor, knees stiff, pins and needles in her right foot. Mrs. Yoder came into the living room, flight of foot. "Do you have any preference for dinner tomorrow?" she asked.

"Whatever you prepare is sure to be a treat," Rachel said.

Ever since they had heard Isaiah was coming home, Mrs. Yoder had been working on making all of his favorite foods.

"Oh! I forgot to mention that some of the folks from the community want to come and see Isaiah."

Mrs. Yoder's eyes widened. Rachel's surprise was unwelcome.

"I can bring some things," Mary piped up. "Adel and I have been baking all week. I can bring some pies and some jams and preserves."

Mrs. Yoder looked relieved. "*Danki* Mary. If you can bring those things, I will make a couple of extra loaves of bread. I'm sure it will be enough for everyone." She said that last sentence as though she were trying to convince herself.

"What time is Isaiah arriving tomorrow?" Mary asked.

"Noah is going to the hospital first thing in the morning to meet Isaiah," Rachel said. "He hopes they will be back by late afternoon."

"That's perfect," Mrs. Yoder exclaimed, clapping her hands together. "It shall be an early dinner then. The weather has been lovely, so perhaps we should set up a table in the garden." The old lady waddled back into the kitchen, murmuring under her breath.

Mary looked across at Rachel, who looked worried.

"Is everything all right?" Mary asked.

Rachel sighed. "I should be happy, and I am, but I don't think I will be truly at ease until Isaiah walks through the front door tomorrow."

"You're worried that something might happen again?"

Rachel nodded. "I know that I shouldn't worry because *Gott* is in control, but, too often, our hopes have been dashed." She lowered her head. "We need Isaiah back so that I can have Noah back."

Isaiah's absence had taken its toll on everyone in a different way. Isaiah had been the one injured, but everyone close to him had paid the price. Rachel had felt that she and Noah had grown apart. The ordeal had revealed to her what people meant when they said that love was not enough. There was no shortness of love in Rachel and Noah's relationship. They had an abundance of love. Their ability to communicate, however, remained underdeveloped.

"I suppose it's useless to tell you not to worry," Mary said. "I'd feel like a hypocrite if I did. Still, worrying doesn't make anything better. It's like rocking in a rocking chair: you'll spend much energy getting nowhere."

Rachel looked at Mary. "When did you become so wise?"

"I wish I were truly wise," Mary said. "I'm lucky to have met someone who's given me some perspective over the last few weeks.

"Adel?" Rachel asked.

Mary nodded.

"*Maem* said you two have been working hard on your home industry?"

"We have," Mary confirmed. "And Mr. Troyer at the general store has helped put us in contact with some *Englischers* who wish to buy from us."

"That is *gut*," Rachel said.

"It's overwhelming," Mary admitted. "Adel came up with the idea only two weeks ago, and we already have orders and customers."

Rachel shook her head in disbelief. Her little sister had grown before her very eyes. "I'm proud of you, *Schweschder*."

"*Danki*. Oh, I wanted to ask you a favor. Could I invite Adel tomorrow?"

Rachel looked surprised but not unhappy.

"It's just she doesn't know many people, and I thought it would be a *gut* chance for her to meet everyone."

"*Ya*," Rachel agreed. "I think that's a fine idea. After all, we'd all like to get to know Adel more and thank her for all of her help."

Thomas came rushing through the doors. "The banner looks *wunderbaar*! You must come and look at it at once."

Both sisters grinned.

"All right," Rachel agreed. "Let's go!"

The next day, the Fishers' front lawn was decorated with a large wooden table bathed in golden light pouring through the leafless trees. Long shadows were cast over the fine Amish furniture. The small party stood near, chatting together. They were all listening closely for the sound of hooves on the road.

Mary had been surprised when she'd seen the Weaver twins, Jacob Beiler, and Hannah King arrive at the Fisher farm.

"What are you doing here?" Mary asked.

"Amos invited me," Abigael said.

"And we asked Rachel if we could come," Sarah explained. "We wanted to see Mr. Fisher."

Mary stood conflicted. They all had, in a minor way, helped raise money for Isaiah, but it had been months ago! Powerless, she nodded. *It's only right they are here to welcome him home,* she reasoned. *I'm glad you're here*, and *I've missed you* were muzzled, lest her vulnerability cause her to collapse. Content with the exchange, she excused herself to look for her sister.

The other teens looked pleasantly surprised. They had expected Mary to be cold toward them. A couple of weeks ago, she would have been.

"What time is it?" Rachel asked.

"It's a little after four," Aaron said.

"I thought that they would be here by now," Rachel admitted. Just as the words left her mouth, they heard horse's hooves against the pavement. A moment later, Noah appeared, alone in the buggy.

Rachel's stomach was in knots.

"He wanted to walk," Noah shouted across to the guests.

What a relief! Rachel thought.

Isaiah was unaware that he had guests waiting. If he had known, he would not have insisted on walking. He yearned for the countryside; its smells, its sights, its freshness, its familiarity. The walk did him good.

"The doctor said to take it easy," Noah had warned.

"The doctor said I could go on short walks," Isaiah had retorted. "I consider the walk from the gate to the house to be short."

Noah had sighed. There was no arguing with the stubborn old man. Plus, he was worn out by chores and farm life. "Fine. The gate to the house, no further."

"You'd think I was asking to climb Kilimanjaro," Isaiah had grumbled.

Noah could not help but grin. It was a relief to have his uncle back and in high spirits, again. When they had arrived at the farm gate, Noah had brought the buggy to a halt, and Isaiah had carefully climbed down. His daily physiotherapy meant that he had regained movement. The doctor had nevertheless warned Isaiah that his leg may never feel the same again. He was to ease himself into his old routine. Isaiah was determined to begin at his earliest convenience.

"I'll see you at the house," Noah had said.

Isaiah had waited for the buggy to disappear over the rise before walking. Should he fall, he did not want his nephew's pity. Should he limp, he wished for a chance to hide it before anyone would know. It was not the stiffness in his leg that dictated Isaiah's speed. It was the ambivalence he felt in his heart. When Isaiah had been driven away in that ambulance, snow had covered the ground. Now, the ground lay littered in a kaleidoscope of autumn leaves. An entire growing season had been lost, his first. His hospital bed had robbed him of a sense of time and place with its monotony of fluorescent tubes and chirping machines. *Oh! Lord, how I am blessed to hear birds, again,* he prayed silently. The sounds of his children's laughter was what he hoped to hear next. His chest ached in grief; his heart skipped with joy.

He was home, at last! Despite losing almost a year, he would live to see another spring, another summer, another fall. He dreaded the thought of another winter.

"How long is he going to take?" Amos groaned.

"Give your *daed* a break," Noah said. "He hasn't been home for seven months."

"I cannot believe you let him walk," Rachel chided.

"No one lets *Onkel* Isaiah do anything. He does what he likes."

No one argued with that one. All now awaited Isaiah's arrival.

"Maybe we should go and look for him?" Mary suggested.

"No, it's okay," Aaron said. "Here, he comes."

Everyone turned as the figure of Isaiah Fisher came into view. He was older and thinner, yet his smile, provoked by the sight of awaiting guests, masked any signs of illness. He looked like a young man again. The twins, Noah, Rachel, and Mary turned to face him, gazing upon him as he made his way home for the first time in over half a year. They watched, mesmerized, as though their relative were a mirage.

Having been elsewhere and, thus, forgotten, Thomas was surprised by the solemnity of the moment and in no way party to it. "*Daed!*" came a shrill shriek of delight from the boy as he tumbled out of the door, burst forth from behind the pack, and sprinted toward his father's open arms. The old man ran forward like the father of the prodigal son, tears blinding him, and only good sense directing him toward a quickly approaching blob. The little boy raced straight into Isaiah's outstretched arms, the pair of which were still sturdy enough to pick him up into the air. Aaron and Amos hurried to regain their father.

"Thomas! You've grown since I last saw you," Isaiah exclaimed.

"I think you're right," Thomas agreed.

"It's *gut* to have you back, *Daed*," Aaron said.

"The place hasn't been the same," Amos added.

"It's good to see you boys," Isaiah said as he looked proudly at his three sons. Thomas was sobbing, whilst the twins' eyes were moist. Isaiah's cup had run over. His joy was complete, his grief left standing at the gate.

The others gave them their space, awaiting their turns to greet Isaiah. Noah shook his uncle's hand firmly when acknowledged, then Rachel and Mary gave him their regards, followed by Mrs. Yoder, who looked at Isaiah's hollow cheeks and shook her head. "We'll soon have you back to your old self."

Noah grinned knowingly at Rachel. The Lapps, Mr. Troyer, and Mr. Stoltzfus brought up the rear. Adel lingered awkwardly near the back of the group.

"Isaiah," Mary said, "this is Adel Raber. She has worked ceaselessly to help me raise funds for your hospital bills. You'll taste her wares shortly."

The pretty, pregnant woman smiled. "Welcome home," Adel said.

"*Danki.*"

When everyone had welcomed Isaiah back, Mrs. Yoder ushered the men to the table. Mary, Rachel, Adel, and Mrs. Lapp went back inside to fetch the food. The men looked on in amazement as they carried out the fresh loaves of bread accompanied by sliced ham with applesauce and roast pork chops with apple chutney. Then came a platter of assorted cheeses, deviled eggs, and plum tomatoes. Alongside the savory delights came the mini peach cobblers, sugar cookies, and *schnitz* pies.

"This is a culinary masterpiece," Isaiah exclaimed. "How did you manage it all Mrs. Yoder?"

"I can't take credit for it all. Mary and Adel made most of the preserves and desserts, and Mrs. Lapp spent all day baking bread."

"Well, I must say this is quite a homecoming."

"Shall we say grace?" Bishop Lapp announced.

Everyone bowed their heads. Isaiah finished first and broke bread. The Fishers' garden had not known such chatter and laughter since Josephine, Isaiah's wife, had passed. Spirits were high. All enjoyed the delicious food in the fading evening light.

When all had eaten their fill and then some, Isaiah cleared his throat. Everyone turned to face him. Isaiah arose, using the table to support himself, and began: "I am not a man of words, but I feel compelled to say something today. As I walked up the road toward the house this afternoon, I tried to find the words to tell you all how much I appreciate what you've done for me over the past seven months. I know that my being gone has affected all of you, and I want to thank you for supporting me, my family, and my nephew's family when I wasn't at my best." Isaiah met Noah's eye. He smiled at him, grateful for his loyalty.

"I thank each and every one here today. To Noah and my boys for looking after our farm, and to Rachel and Mrs. Yoder for looking after everyone." He paused for the laughter. "I am thankful to Bishop Lapp, who came to me at my darkest time and showed me the path back to the light, and to Mrs. Lapp, who never forgot my love of chicken corn soup. It made me feel as if I were back home."

Mrs. Lapp blushed at the mention of her name.

"I owe a debt of thanks to Mr. Troyer and Mr. Stoltzfus, who showed a depth of generosity and compassion that I have not often witnessed in my life."

Both men also looked quite flustered by Isaiah's words of praise.

"And last, but certainly not least, I am abundantly thankful to Mary and all the gardeners who so many months ago wanted to help me. Although they may have had very little knowledge of gardening when they first began, their compassion, spirit, and heart were sufficient to see it grow into a success. Over the seasons, I kept track of the garden's progress and the stories that unfolded along the way. I want you to know that garden was my refuge during the bad days. It was the place I'd go when I closed my eyes. I'd imagine myself standing under the dogwood tree listening to a summer storm or planting pumpkin seeds in the freshly dug earth."

Mary looked around the table in amazement. She had no idea that Isaiah had followed their progress so closely.

"Your garden helped me in ways that none of us would have expected, and there is no way I can ever repay you all for what you did."

Noah suddenly stood up. "I hate to interrupt, but I think this is the perfect time to announce that with the money from the harvest so far, as well as the funds raised from the garden and Adel and Mary's home industry, we have managed to get on top of all of the hospital bills."

There were gasps, looks of amazement, then applause, not for the youths, but for God who, in His mercy, had taken care of His child. The women clutched at their hearts for fear that they would flutter away.

"*Gott* is *gut*," Bishop Lapp announced.

There were cheers of agreement.

Mary's heart swelled as she looked around at all the gardeners. They had all done more than they had set out to do. They had also found more than they had expected.

* * *

It took Isaiah no time to settle back into his life on the farm. He had worried that the time in the hospital had been too long, but he had not forgotten the farm's ways. His old lifestyle fit like a well-worn pair of jeans. His third day home was the first morning Noah, Rachel, and Mrs. Yoder agreed that he could do some work. Their henpecking had driven him mad. "Has anyone seen my hat?"

"It should be in your room," Noah said.

"I usually leave it on the hook," Isaiah explained, "but it isn't there anymore."

Noah frowned.

"What's wrong?" Rachel asked as she came into the kitchen with Jo on her hip. Jo immediately put her arms out to Isaiah, and he took her.

"*Onkel* Isaiah can't find his hat," Noah explained.

"Oh," Rachel said, "about that…"

Thomas walked into the kitchen wearing a straw hat covering his eyes.

"Thomas, is that my hat?"

Thomas looked at his father with round, innocent eyes. "Oh no, this is my hat."

Isaiah raised his eyebrows, waiting for an explanation.

"I didn't want your hat to feel lonely while you were gone because it didn't have a head to wear it, so I adopted it. I wear it on my head, which is like your head but smaller."

"You adopted my hat?"

"I think it looks quite *gut* on me."

Noah exhaled as though he were holding back a sneeze. It was all it took for Rachel to giggle uncontrollably.

"*Danki,* Tommy, for looking after my hat while I was gone."

"I suppose you want it back?" Thomas asked, bottom lip quivering. He'd make a puppy dog sad.

Isaiah hesitated, then shook his head. "No, I think you should keep it. It does look *gut* on you."

Thomas beamed, then headed outside. As he turned, his hat fell entirely over his eyes. He bumped into the doorframe.

"Be careful," Isaiah called out.

"So, what's your plan for today?" Noah asked.

"Well, I suppose I need to get a new hat," Isaiah said.

Noah and Rachel chuckled.

"We do need some things from the supply store," Noah said. "I wasn't sure you were ready to drive the buggy again."

Isaiah sighed. He wasn't sure if he was ready either. "I'll be fine. I'll go into town after breakfast and get what we need." He said it more to convince himself than the others.

Isaiah was in no hurry to get to town. Breakfast was a good excuse to delay his excursion without having to admit that he was nervous. A slow drive would get him used to being back in the buggy, driving. He mounted the carriage with a belly full of breakfast and butterflies. When he passed the King farm, he spotted something strange. At first, he thought it was an animal. As he got closer, he realized that it was a person lying on the side of the road. Isaiah picked up speed.

"Are you okay?" Isaiah shouted. He didn't wait for a reply before he climbed down from the buggy. Isaiah walked around the side of the buggy and recognized Adel's pale face peering out from under her *kapp*.

"Adel! What's happened?"

"It's too soon," Adel gasped.

"What is it? What can I do?"

Adel groaned, inhaled deeply, collected herself, then said, as calmly as she could, "The baby is coming. But it's too soon. It's not time." She was panting. Sweat covered her forehead and cheeks. She'd been lying there for a while.

"What do we do?"

Adel looked at the man in the eyes. "I very much don't want to have my baby on the side of the road. Perhaps, you could take me to the hospital?"

"The hospital? *Ya*, of course." Isaiah bent over to help Adel to her feet. She was breathing heavily. She made it up into the buggy. He climbed up beside her. Grabbing the reins, Isaiah yelled, and the horse started quickly down the road. As they went, Adel seemed to be getting worse and her breathing, labored.

"I'm sorry," Adel said.

"For what?" Isaiah asked

"I'm sure that the hospital is the last place on earth you wish to visit again."

Isaiah laughed dryly. She was not wrong. Still, the hospital was better than delivering a baby in a buggy. "May I ask why you are going to the hospital?"

Birthing was a woman's business, but even Isaiah knew that

Amish women did not like to go to the hospital to deliver their babies. They liked to have them at home, where they would be comfortable and safe, and where nature and God could take the lead.

"The baby is early," Adel explained. "I think by eight or nine weeks. I'm scared that maybe it's too early. I know that maybe it is not our way, but I cannot lose this baby, Isaiah. I will not lose it." She was desperate. As though sensing her plight, the horse picked up the pace.

Often, babies who come too early do not survive. It is the way of the Amish to allow them to return to God. Still, Isaiah could not blame Adel for wanting to do right by her baby. Before Thomas was born, Josephine had had three miscarriages. The grief had nearly killed Isaiah. When he'd found Jo was pregnant again, he'd done everything in his power to ensure they would not suffer another lost baby. Thomas was their miracle baby.

"I hope you don't judge me," Adel said, "for choosing to go and deliver my baby at the hospital. I trust *Gott*, but this baby is all that I have left of my husband. A little bit of help from the doctors couldn't hurt."

"I understand," Isaiah said. "More than you know. On my wife's deathbed, I promised her that I would keep our *sohs* safe. Then, last year, Thomas fell into a frozen lake and became terribly ill. I did not want him to go to the hospital because my wife had died in the hospital, and I could not reconcile my anger and distrust with modern medicine. I was stubborn, and Thomas almost died because of it. Even after spending months in the hospital, I do not like modern medicine, but I have learned to appreciate that it has its place in the world. Maybe even in the *Amisch* community."

Adel groaned loudly, clutching her side.

"We are almost there," Isaiah promised.

Once at the hospital, Adel was unable to walk, such were her labor pains. Isaiah hurried through the large glass doors to fetch a nurse and a wheelchair. They quickly wheeled her into the hospital.

"Who do we have here?" a doctor asked.

"This is Adel Raber, female, age twenty-three, thirty-four weeks pregnant," the nurse answered.

"Thirty-four weeks?"

Adel nodded. "That's my best guess."

Upon a quick examination, the doctor declared, "She's in raging labor. Let's get her ready for delivery."

The nurses rushed into action, moving Adel to a delivery room, gearing up with gowns and gloves, and then preparing monitors and an incubator. Isaiah looked at the action before him, and when Adel was whisked away, his head spun, unsure of what to do. A slender nurse grabbed his arm. "Come on, Dad." Isaiah gasped and grunted in a pathetic attempt to formulate an objection, too shocked to correct her. He tried not to walk, but she was stronger than she looked. She yanked him into step with her, looked back at him with determination on the cusp of disappointment, and declared, "She needs you." Isaiah relented since she was unlikely to take kindly to any more resistance.

Adel seemed unaware. Her face was pale, she clenched the sides of the bed in mid-contraction, and her eyes widened. No reasonable soul would leave her alone with utter strangers at such a time as this. Isaiah acquiesced. He would pretend to be the father just so that she would not be by herself.

It was a surreal experience to hold the hand of a woman

Isaiah had met only three days prior while she birthed her first-born. They shared a moment, normally reserved for long-time lovers, on their first date. A better location could have been picked for the occasion, and one not so crowded. Nevertheless, they got to know each other quickly. Adel did all the talking and commanded all the attention, while he listened and acted to make her wishes reality. It was idyllic in that sense, for how many women would reject a man who actually listened? Indeed, when Isaiah did not know what to do, he asked for directions to make sure he did things correctly. With him, Adel's comfort and well-being were secure.

Throughout, Isaiah wanted to tell the truth, that he wasn't the baby's father, that he hardly knew Adel, but the poor woman had no one else. How would she feel when confronted with her solitude holding the only living souvenir of her dearly departed husband? Who else could be there? The Amish had no quick means of communication. Then it dawned on him: Adel had lost her husband, moved to a new town, and volunteered to help a man she did not know: himself. Now she was having a baby. She was going to need him. Isaiah's disdain for hospitals never occurred to him.

An eruption of adult jubilation and the piercing shrill of an infant's first cry announced the end of the ordeal and the beginning of a magical time. Adel groaned. Isaiah looked at her as though looking through a windshield in a thunderstorm. It did not occur to him to use his wipers.

"Keep pushing, Momma. We gotta get the rest out."

Adel moaned her displeasure.

"Dad? It's a girl."

Isaiah blinked. He could not see who had addressed him.

"Is she okay?" Adel exhaled.

"She's fine," the doctor reassured her.

"Here are the scissors, Dad. Come cut the umbilical cord."

Isaiah couldn't see for the tears. As one nurse aggressively called for him to cut the cord, Adel had the wherewithal to reach for a tissue. "Here, Isaiah. Wipe your eyes."

Now, the farmer looked less like he was fumbling about in the darkness. He reached forth and did the honor usually reserved for the father: cutting the umbilical cord. The baby lay still on her mother's chest.

"Look at her," Isaiah said to Adel. "She looks…" He paused, trying to find the right word.

"Purple?" Adel ventured. She was resplendent. Isaiah wanted to look at the baby, but Adel's gaze and sense of humor captivated him. He was smitten.

CHAPTER 5: UNEXPECTED VISITORS

The baby was named "Leora," and the week following her birth was as eventful as her arrival into the world. The story of how Isaiah had found the widow alone on the side of the road while in labor quickly became the talk of the town. People were amazed by Isaiah's dedication to the newcomer, and, while no one could quite understand it, there was no doubting something extraordinary had happened. It began once Adel was ready to return home with the baby two days after her birth.

"I know that you want to do this alone," Isaiah said, "but you are part of our community now, and we want to help you."

Adel was worried about what people might say or assume. There was a noble dignity to a widow, less so for a spinster, single mom. She felt that Isaiah's position could not be jeopardized nor could doubt be cast upon his character. The Amish are a forgiving lot, but they do talk. The last thing she needed was to be dragged before the elders and shunned just as she was getting back up on her feet. Furthermore, friends were hard to come by; she could not afford to alienate the Fishers for their act of kindness.

"Aren't you worried about what people might say?" Adel asked.

"No," Isaiah said plainly. "We have done nothing to be ashamed of, and I believe that Rachel, Mrs. Yoder, and I could be a help and comfort to you during these early days."

The chance to have a support system around at such a vulnerable time outweighed the risks of perceived impropriety. Adel agreed. She wrapped Leora snugly in a blanket and carried her out to where Isaiah awaited to take them home.

"Welcome back," Mrs. Yoder exclaimed back at the farm even before the buggy had come to a stop. She immediately put her arms out for Adel to give her the sleeping baby. "She's beautiful, just beautiful," she whispered, utterly enamored. She kissed the baby on the forehead and turned to take her inside. The older woman carried Leora into the house, leaving Rachel to help Adel up the stairs.

"*Danki*," Adel said, "for welcoming Leora and me into your home. I know that this is extra work for someone whom you hardly know."

"Don't be silly," Rachel said. "We can't wait to have a new little person in the house. Besides, any friend of my sister is a friend of mine." Rachel stayed mum, however, about using Leora to warm Noah up to the idea of another child.

"It's a relief to have others around to help," Adel admitted. "I'd been wondering how I was going to do it in a new place. Your family warmly embracing me and my baby is an answer to prayer."

Rachel didn't know what to say, so she showed Adel the way to her room at the end of the hall. A beautiful bay window overlooked the back garden. "It's going to be a bit squished, but we hope you will be comfortable here until you are ready to go back home."

In the corner of the room was the bed, made with fresh linen. Next to the bed was a Moses basket in which Leora could sleep. There were fresh towels and a clean bowl of water on the table by the door. Someone had even left a vase of garden roses on the nightstand.

"This is perfect," Adel said.

Rachel smiled. "I know how overwhelming it can be to have a newborn. I can't imagine doing it without the help of other women. So you can count on us."

Adel put her hand over her heart. She had lost her mother when she was just a girl and her father shortly after she was wed. Daniel had been the only family she had left until the accident.

"I was so sure that I could do it on my own," Adel said, "but the reality is much scarier than I imagined. If I hadn't had Isaiah with me, I don't know if Leora would be here."

"You are braver than you know," Rachel objected. "It does not hurt to have a hand to hold when things are hard. You can do this."

"I worry that I put Isaiah in an uncomfortable position."

"Isaiah is not a man who allows himself to be led unwillingly," Rachel reassured the new mother. "He was with you in that hospital room because that's where he wanted to be. He is a man of honor. It was the right thing to do."

Adel felt relieved by Rachel's assurance. Ever since Leora's birth, she had worried that Isaiah might resent her for putting him in such a bind.

"Now, make yourself at home," Rachel instructed. "You've had a long day. I'll call you when supper is ready."

Adel nodded. She closed the door softly, retreated to the small bed, and lay down. Heavy eyes and a soft pillow lulled her fast asleep.

The next two days flew by. Despite the close quarters, the group became tightly knit, largely due to Leora being a good baby. Mrs. Yoder was oft delayed for wanting to hold her in the rocking chair for "just a few more minutes." Rachel held her in front of Noah at every opportunity as though her new baby smell would make him yearn for another one of his own. The twins and Thomas were intrigued, but boys are hardly interested in babies. Even Josephine was largely ignored by them, not out of menace but simply by nature. Except for Adel, no one adored Leora as much as Isaiah did. He had always been a dedicated father, and he now shared this dedication with the little girl. He sang her lullabies, called her nicknames, and was very much attached to her.

It was on Leora's fifth day, when Adel and Rachel were hanging up the washing in the back yard in the middle of Indian summer, as she lay fast asleep in her Moses basket under a nearby tree, that Mrs. Yoder joined them, looking grim.

"Adel," Mrs. Yoder called from the kitchen, "you have visitors."

Adel frowned. It could not be Mary because she would not be so formal. She had no other close friends.

"Go," Rachel said. "I'll keep an eye on Leora."

"They are in the sitting room," Mrs. Yoder said. "I'll bring you all some tea."

Adel walked down the narrow hallway and into the sitting room. When she saw her visitors, she stopped dead. "What are you doing here?"

In the Fisher sitting room was a middle-aged couple. The

woman was used to having her own way, and the man next to her was the one who saw to it that she did. Adel's ire was directed at the slender, thick-browed, woman dressed in a black Amish dress and *kapp*. Her eyes were of the coldest blue. Her lips were indiscernible in color from the rest of her face were it not for a thin mustache at its edges, though she did not look foolish. To the contrary, if there were an Amish mafia, it's godfather would have dispatched her to slip a horse's head into his rival's bed in the middle of the night. She returned Adel's gaze and did not rise to meet her. "We've come to meet our *enkelin* (granddaughter)."

How her in-laws had managed to learn that Leora had been born and where she was staying, Adel did not wish to know. For whoever it was who told them would suffer vengeance like none had witnessed since Parysatis avenged Cyrus. "How did you know?"

"That is unimportant," interjected Mr. Raber. His was a deep, melancholic voice resonating with authority, commanding and strong, and finished with a bitter note of yearning to be loosed from his chain. He was a formidable man—an intimidating one, even—whose long, unkempt beard flowed over his barrel-chest. Warm, green eyes looked over spectacles to Adel, and the girl wondered how warm, compassionate Daniel could have sprung from the loins of such an imposing man and his miserable wife.

Adel looked at the otherwise pleasant face of her father-in-law, pleasant for his presage as to what his son's would have looked like had he survived to live into his fifties. The only thing the two had in common was a most unusual shade of green eyes. She hesitated. Suddenly, the morning that she had left came rushing back to her. Adel had told her in-laws that she was going, but neither had taken her seriously until they had seen her luggage packed and the train ticket clutched tightly in her hand.

"You're leaving?" Mr. Raber had asked.

"I told you I was going," Adel had reminded him.

"Jonathan, you cannot let her go," Mrs. Raber had pleaded desperately with her husband.

"Adel, you are grieving. You are not thinking clearly. Daniel would never agree to you taking our unborn *kinnskind* (grandchild) away. He believed that family was the most important thing in the world."

"You don't need to tell me what my husband believed," Adel had snapped. "I am not some mad widow with no sense. I know what I am doing."

"Just come back to the house with us, and we'll make some tea and talk about this," Mrs. Raber had suggested.

"I am not going back into the house; I have a train to catch." Adel had turned her back on the Rabers. To date, it was the boldest thing she had ever done. She had neither seen nor heard from them in nigh-on three months. Yet, there they stood before her, the pair of them returning unexpectedly at the most inconvenient of times.

"May we see our *enkelin*?" Mrs. Raber asked, returning Adel to the present.

Adel stuttered with her feet, at once trying to flee, return to her daughter, and show the Rabers the door out.

"Please," Mrs. Raber whispered. "We've come all this way."

Adel finally exhaled, knowing that she could not keep Leora away from them forever. "Wait here." She headed outside and found Leora still sound asleep.

"Who is it?" Rachel asked.

"My in-laws," Adel explained.

Rachel stopped moving, sensing the air for predators. "What do they want?"

"They want to meet Leora." Adel picked up the infant basket and returned to her relatives. "She's asleep."

Mrs. and Mr. Raber approached for their first glimpse at their sleeping granddaughter and their beloved son's only offspring. Sadness, grief, and joy could all be countenanced, to varying degrees, on each of their faces.

"She's beautiful," Mrs. Raber whispered.

Leora stirred, then opened her eyes. Both Mr. and Mrs. Raber gasped and said, in unison, "It's impossible."

Newborns of European stock are often born with blue eyes that later change color. Leora, however, had been born with the exact shade of viridian green of her grandfather and father. The child's value, it seemed, went from one cherished, to one prized. "May I hold her?" Mrs. Raber asked as though begging to hold some fine porcelain.

Adel handed her to the older woman.

"We don't even know her name," Mr. Raber stated.

That's because you didn't ask, thought Adel. "Leora," Adel spat, immediately regretting saying her daughter's name as though it were venom on her tongue. It had been Daniel's idea.

"Leora?" Adel had asked. "It sounds nice, but why?"

"Because she will be the light that fills our hearts and the one that burns the brightest."

Adel had agreed, knowing full well that her in-laws would be particularly displeased, but assuming that her late husband would bear the brunt of their indignation.

Predictably, Mr. Raber frowned. "Did you even consider giving her a family name?"

"Leora is the name that Daniel chose," Adel said, trying not to look smug.

Mr. Raber said no more but continued to look unhappy. Adel thanked the Lord that the old man held his tongue. Just as the uncomfortable silence reached its apex, Leora fussed.

"She's hungry," Adel explained, holding out her hands.

Mrs. Raber begrudgingly handed Leora back to her mother. Adel sought privacy in the kitchen. Mrs. Yoder entered from the kitchen with tea and biscuits.

"I'm just going to feed Leora," Adel told her.

"Take your time, dear," Mrs. Yoder said, seeing her pinched expression. She presumed it was the company—and not constipation—that made the new mother grimace.

Adel was relieved for a moment alone, away from the horrible people responsible for her wonderful husband. She sat in a chair by the window and brought Leora to her breast. As the baby suckled contently, Adel listened to the murmured voices from the living room.

"We love having Adel and Leora here," Mrs. Yoder said. "They are such a pleasure, no trouble at all."

Adel smiled gratefully at the kind words.

"And who are you exactly?" Mr. Raber asked.

"I am the Fishers' neighbor, but I help out with the cooking and cleaning."

"So, you are not a member of the family, then." Silence followed Mr. Raber's statement, and Adel gritted her teeth.

"Well, no, but I've helped out the Fishers for so long I may as well be." Mrs. Yoder giggled. "I've helped raise Thomas since he was just a day old. It wasn't in *Gott's* plan to give me children, so He gave me the Fishers instead."

"Well, you seem to get attached to any child but your own," said Mrs. Raber. "This is a funny way to ensure the proper care of children. I suppose this community is ready to take in any stray who wanders past. How come these Fisher boys don't have their *groosseldre* care for them? Where we come from, family takes care of their own."

"Perhaps you can put in a word to Adel to let her see the wisdom of our ways," enjoined Mr. Raber, "lest our *enkelin* suffer the fate of these Fisher boys and not know her family."

A weighty silence followed, and before Mrs. Yoder spoke, Adel felt a tremor in the earth. Only upon collecting herself so as to avoid a vocable eruption did the old woman venture a rebuttal. "I am certain Adel would appreciate no such thing coming from me because, in our community, we don't ask others to take care of our business." She swiftly arose and returned to the kitchen. "Good luck with those two," she grumbled to Adel.

"I'm sorry if they were rude to you," Adel apologized.

"You have nothing to apologize for," Mrs. Yoder said. "I can see now why you thought you had to leave and begin again. Two minutes in a room with them, and I was ready to pack a bag."

Adel smiled. Mrs. Yoder was certainly a card. That dreaded moment when Leora was satisfied and she would be forced to return to the living room, neared. Adel burped her a little longer than usual to forestall the inevitable. Her in-laws were not going to leave soon after coming a long way. Furthermore, they were not people who dealt well with disappointment. They would tirelessly harangue her to get their way, thus avoiding any type of setback and its requisite feelings. Her marriage to Daniel was probably the only thing they had ever let slip past them, and they begrudged her. Adel's anxiety balled up in her chest, threatening to asphyxiate her. *If only Daniel were here,* she thought, *he could fend them off.* She looked up to the heavens, pleading with the Lord to take this cup away from her. No solace came. Her breathing was shallow. Panic would soon set in. She thought of taking the baby and running. *My baby!* Adel looked down at Leora. In her face she found courage. She knew why she had left the suffocating grip of the Rabers and what she had to do for her daughter, and she could finally breathe again. Should a person ever feel overwhelmed with indecision, doubt, and uncertainty, she need only look into the face of a newborn baby. Indeed, it is impossible to remember the problems of this world whilst being scrutinized by such utter innocence. When this delicate being finds its only protection in the might of the hands in which it rests, the furnace of the soul is lit, and its ember-glow burns in the guardian's eyes.

Adel was thrust back to reality by voices in the living room. Mrs. Yoder now stood near the kitchen window, so it could not be her addressing the Rabers. She left her chair, convinced that whoever it was would also need saving from the monsters-in-law. Isaiah stood in the center of the room.

"Isaiah," Adel said. "These are Mr. and Mrs. Raber."

"*Ya*," Isaiah said, "we've just been introduced." He gritted his teeth to convey his displeasure with the introductions.

"They came to meet Leora," Adel explained.

"Well, they have met Leora, so perhaps they should go." Only after he had made his declaration did he turn to his unwelcome guests.

Adel had not known Isaiah to be so forthright. It was chilling yet reassuring at the same time. She made a note to remain on his warmer side.

"We've also traveled all this way to ask Adel to come home,"

Mr. Raber said.

"Adel and Leora live here now," Isaiah snapped. "They have a home and a family with us."

Mr. Raber frowned. "We can see you are in the habit of picking up strays, but this is a family matter. We'd appreciate it if you stayed out of it."

Isaiah paused before formulating his next sentence like a good Amish man. Though his intent was to carefully think about what he would say next and say it in a manner akin to Christ, it only served the man to make his already sharp remarks more incisive. He pointed to Adel's in-laws. "You should be so fortunate that I let strays wander into my living room with 'family matters.' If you had handled your affairs while Adel was still in your community, I would not have to be so inconvenienced." Adel put her hand on his arm.

"Isaiah," she murmured, "will you take Leora outside and give us a moment, please?" She quickly thrust the newborn into his arms. It was a delight to watch him melt whenever he held the little one. Truly, if he were lost with the girl, one would need only to find the puddle from where he first held her, then follow his wet footsteps to where he carried her.

Adel and Daniel's parents were alone again in the sitting room. Adel took a deep breath. Looking directly at the imposing patriarch, she announced, "I am not going back with you. I've built a new life here for myself. I have friends, and Leora has people who love her and can care for her."

"You have all of that back home," Mr. Raber boomed. "These people are not your family, Adel. We are your family, and we deserve to be part of our *enkelin's* life."

"I am not going back," Adel repeated.

"You are selfish," Mr. Raber snapped. "Have you ever thought about what Daniel would have wanted? Or Leora? You have always been a self-centered girl, and your actions now are proof that you don't care for Daniel's wishes or his family." His words slapped Adel across the face.

Mrs. Raber chimed in in a vulturous tone. "I know that we have never been close, but surely you would not deny us the chance to be close to Leora, to love and care for her as *groosseldre* are supposed to? You cannot hate us that much."

Adel balled her fists, clenched her jaw, and shut her eyes. Her throat burned, damming the salty rush to her eyes, threatening to dissolve in a saline wave. She inhaled sharply through her nose. "I think you should go. Now."

"Humph," uttered Mr. Raber. He strode past her without giving her another look.

Mrs. Raber turned around at the door. "We aren't leaving yet. We will return to fetch you. Please be ready when we do."

CHAPTER 6: I HAVE LIGHT

Adel did not know where her feet were carrying her. Leora was safe with Isaiah, which meant she could leave the house. Unconsciously, she walked, seeing only images in her mind's eye of Leora, Daniel's face, Isaiah cutting the umbilical cord, and Mary's smile when she canned and cooked at her place. She knew not where her feet were carrying her, only that she trusted them to take her where her heart needed to be.

Adel stopped at the small gate leading to the garden. Her burden was lighter. Peace beckoned her from beyond the gate. She pushed open the gate, and it gave her its rusty welcome. Her feet led straight to the small, stone bench at the end of the garden, her favorite haunt for sitting and feeling.

Mary was on her way to the Fisher farm, taking an unusual route through a grassy meadow since she felt like rambling. On the road, she spotted a familiar-looking figure. Had she been closer, Mary would have called out to Adel, but she was too far, and the breeze was blowing in the wrong direction. Adel seemed to be in an awful hurry. Mary wondered if she and Adel had plans to meet in the garden. One more look at the new mother cautioned Mary to stay true to her course. All would be revealed in time. She tracked Adel until she was out of sight, then regained her path to her sister's abode.

At the Fisher farm, Mary found Rachel, Noah, and Isaiah, who was holding Leora, standing on the front porch. They seemed to be enjoying the horizon. It was only upon approach that she could hear their hushed tones.

"Nobody saw where she went?" Isaiah asked, his tone terse.

"No," Rachel answered. "She was in the living room, and then she just disappeared."

"It's unlike her," Isaiah said.

Noah raised his eyebrows.

"What?" Isaiah said defensively.

"Well, it's not as if any one of us knows her very well."

"I know her well enough to know she wouldn't just leave Leora, not unless there was a very good reason."

"I saw Adel," Mary said as she climbed up the porch steps. They all collectively jumped; no one had seen her coming. "Just a few minutes ago. She was hurrying toward the garden."

Isaiah breathed a sigh of relief. "I need to go and talk to her." He stepped forward and handed the baby to Mary, who had not been expecting the privilege. Once secured, Mary cooed and smiled at the child, paying the rest no heed.

"Maybe you should give her some time," Noah suggested.

Isaiah shook his head. As he made his way to the garden, he rehearsed what he was going to say to Adel. When he had walked into the house earlier that day and found her in-laws seated on the couch, it had unnerved him. Adel had told him that she had no family of her own, except for Daniel's parents. Isaiah had thought them estranged. When Mr. Raber had then asked Adel to go back to her old community, the request had chafed him. The idea of Adel leaving with Leora crushed him. He was determined to convince her to stay in Erie.

Once in the garden, Isaiah made his way down the narrow paths between the beds in search of Adel. He finally saw her seated on the old stone bench. She had her head down and did not see him approaching. It was only when Isaiah stood right in front of her that Adel looked up at him.

"How did you find me?" Adel asked.

"Mary spotted you on the road."

Adel did not respond.

"May I sit?" Met only with silence, Isaiah helped himself. "Why did you run?"

"It's complicated," Adel managed.

"Is it because the Rabers asked you to go back?"

Adel nodded.

"You don't have to go. You can stay with me—with us—for as long as you want."

"That is a kind offer," Adel said, "but I think the Rabers might be right. Perhaps it is time for me to return home."

"I don't understand," Isaiah exclaimed. "I thought you were happy here."

"I am. I never thought that I would know happiness again after Daniel's death, but then I met Mary and all of you, and I felt as if I had found somewhere to belong."

"Then why do you want to leave?"

"Because I fear that if I stay, it may be for the wrong reasons," Adel admitted. "The Rabers have asked me to return, and perhaps it is the best thing for Leora. They are her *groosseldre*, after all."

"What's best for you?" Isaiah was pleading rather than asking. "By all means, allow the Rabers to be a part of Leora's life, but don't do it at the expense of your own happiness and everything that you have gained since arriving here."

"It's not just about me anymore, Isaiah. I have to do the right thing for Leora."

That was unexpected.

"What if I am the right thing?" Isaiah asked. Adel looked astonished. "What if I am the right thing for you and Leora?"

"Isaiah!"

"I was raised in a home where my parents could barely tolerate each other. I didn't expose my boys to that. I loved Josephine to her dying day, then I raised them alone because I thought that I could never again meet someone with whom I'd get along. Your in-laws are monsters! Do you really want them that close to you and your baby? Do you see yourselves getting along? If Daniel's not here to get along with you, then let me! Let Leora grow up in a home with joy." He stopped as tears welled up in his eyes.

Adel sat quietly, mesmerized by the spectacle. This man had found her bent in pain on the side of the road, and now he was ready to carry her over the threshold. When she looked down to his forearm, she found her hand already there.

"I know this is sudden, and maybe you think that I am crazy, but I know what I want, and I've never been wrong about a person. You are exceptional, Adel, in every way possible. I'd like the opportunity of loving you from now until the day *Gott* calls me home."

The pair blubbered, giggled, and cried a while. Nowhere had a stone bench ever been warmer, and no dusk ever more radiant. Surely, it was because of the brightness of their smiles.

"For a man of few words, you are quite versed at stringing

them together," Adel finally said.

"Only when it counts," Isaiah replied. "So, what do you think?"

Adel took a deep breath before looking Isaiah in the eye.

"I think that any woman would be lucky to have your love. I don't think that you are crazy. The truth is that I was drawn to you before I met you. When Mary told me the story of your accident, it sounded so much like what had happened to my Daniel. But unlike him, you survived. I knew that moment, indeed, that I would do everything I could to help you. I wish I could say that my motives were entirely selfless, but they weren't. Your accident helped me to heal. Through helping you, I was able to work through those feelings of guilt and uselessness I felt when Daniel died. Then, when I met you at your homecoming dinner, I was surprised by how much I liked you. I told my heart to stop it. I had convinced myself I was done with love. After all, people rarely get one great love in their life, so why should I think I might be deserving of two? I tried to push my attraction for you away and thought I had succeeded."

"Until I met you on the roadside," Isaiah added.

"Exactly," Adel agreed, smiling. She wiped away a tear of joy. "There I was in labor, and who should come along but you. I wanted you there. I wanted it to be you. I was glad they assumed you were my husband at the hospital. When you held Leora for the first time, you beamed with adoration and love. I wanted so much for her *daed* to be there, but he wasn't. Since then, we've become entangled in each other's lives. While I love every minute with you, I am reminded that Daniel is dead whenever you are around." Adel's words hung in the air before disappearing on the wind.

"So, what are you saying?"

"I think what I am trying to say is that I love you, Isaiah, but the love is not pure. It is conflicted and unrefined. Daniel is still with me. I haven't let him go."

Isaiah nodded. He understood that there was no finite amount of time it took to move on from someone you loved. He could not hold it against her.

"*Danki*, for being honest with me," Isaiah said. "I can understand that there is no set amount of time to move forward from such a loss." Isaiah got up. "I hope to still be friends."

"Wait," Adel interjected, "I don't want to be friends."

"Then, what do you propose?"

"I was hoping that you would wait for me."

Isaiah grinned. "Of course, I'll wait for you."

"I don't know how long it'll take. Are you sure you want to?"

"I'm a patient man."

When Adel looked into Isaiah's eyes, the world slowed down. Then, a pile of leaves beside them erupted in an ecstatic roar. Adel let out a piercing scream. Childish laughter echoed about the garden. Thomas had managed to infiltrate their sanctum unnoticed.

"Thomas!" Isaiah cried. "What are you doing? You nearly gave us a heart attack!"

"Sorry," Thomas mumbled. "I thought it would be funny."

Adel and Isaiah both stood covered in leaves.

"How did you even crawl into that pile of leaves without us noticing?" Isaiah asked.

Thomas shrugged. "You two were so busy talking that you didn't see me. I did a leopard crawl across the whole garden."

Isaiah shook his head. He was doing his best not to laugh.

"Are you sure you want to get involved in my family?"

"Oh, absolutely," Adel chuckled as she removed a leaf from Isaiah's beard.

* * *

Adel invited the Rabers over to the house for tea on the morrow. She had thought long and hard about what she was going to say to them. When they arrived, Adel reintroduced them into the living room. In a show of good faith, she handed Leora to Mrs. Raber.

"*Danki*, for coming," Adel said. "I thought hard about our meeting yesterday, and while I appreciate you both coming all the way here to meet Leora, I am afraid I will not return with you."

Mr. Raber opened his mouth, but Adel did not stop to breathe.

"When Daniel died, I went searching for some way to find myself again, and I met a young woman by the name of Mary. She invited me into her life without knowing a single thing about me. Mary's friendship opened a door for me, and soon I found myself surrounded by people who truly cared for me. While I know you both love Leora, moving back would not be the right decision for either of us. We all loved Daniel, but the truth is that we will never love one another."

"Adel, you must understand that we care for you," Mrs. Raber said.

"That is kind of you to say, Mrs. Raber, even if you do not mean it."

"So, what does this mean for Leora and us?" Mr. Raber asked coldly.

"Daniel would have wanted his *dochder* to know her *groosseldre*, so you are welcome to visit her here."

Mr. and Mrs. Raber shared a look. Her mother-in-law then spoke up. "Adel, we are family. It is proper for us to care for her and to bond with her in her youth. Her place is with us."

"Her place is with me. If you wish to be nearer to her, you are welcome to move to Erie."

"My farm has been in my family for generations," said Mr. Raber. "You expect me to sell it?"

"I expect you to do what you will. My understanding from yesterday is that your concern is for Leora. You know where she lives, and you are free to visit."

"Daniel would want you near us."

"Daniel isn't here. If he were, he would want me near him. At present, I speak for my family, and I have spoken."

Mrs. Raber looked into her grandchild's face. She seemed to have excused herself from the conversation, hardly noticing the repartee before her. Only Leora commanded her attention.

"I think we can respect your wishes," Mrs. Raber said.

"Ha!" retorted her husband. "*Familye*! It is us who are to raise her in our ways! Who will teach her humility, selflessness, devotion to our *Ordnung*? These strangers?"

"Indeed," Adel said. "This is an *Amisch* community."

"A community that leaves its child-rearing to strangers and neighbors! Bah!"

Adel fixed her jaw and stared coldly at Daniel's father. Though he held all the authority as the patriarch of an Amish household, there was little fight left now that his wife had been turned. The widow's strategy had worked; the woman had come to see the child, while the man had come to impose his will. Once divided, he would have little incentive to continue without an ally. Though he may never recant his demand, Adel could rest assured that his present offensive would fizzle.

Mrs. Raber looked satisfied. She stood up and handed Leora to Adel. "Well, now that that is all sorted, we have a train to catch. Goodbye, Leora. We will see you soon."

"Goodbye, Mrs. Raber, Mr. Raber," Adel said.

Mr. Raber pouted, arose, looked sternly at Adel, then glided swiftly out of the house.

Mrs. Raber lingered in her husband's wake. "Losing Daniel has been hard for Mr. Raber. He is not usually a cold man."

Mr. Raber has never been warmer than freezing, Adel thought. Unwilling to forestall their departure, Adel remained mute as her mother-in-law left. Adel stood watching on the front porch, with Leora sleeping snuggly in her arm.

"Are they gone?" Isaiah asked.

"They've just left," Adel said.

"How did it go?"

"As well as could be expected."

"I'll be here when they visit her, you know, if you want me to."

Adel said nothing.

"Only if you want me to. If it's too soon, then I understand."

"I think I'd like that," Adel whispered.

CHAPTER 7: ASHES

The garden's trees stood bare of their leaves, lightened from their summer burden, yet geriatric in the noises they made in the late autumn breeze. Groans and grinds echoed about the space; bare branches turned to crackling windchimes. The skeleton of each deciduous tree was an annual reminder that all life ends in death. Soon, frost would coat them in a glistening glaze. The last days of autumn were upon Mary and her friends.

Mary was busy preparing the garden for winter, alone. It would be the first frost that her garden would know, so she wanted it to be ready. She had underestimated the amount of work it would be. It had taken her the better part of a week to prepare. Adel, being preoccupied with Leora, and Isaiah, busy winterizing his own farm and making the necessary preparations for his son's wedding, had, nevertheless, given a list of instructions on how to best prepare the garden for winter.

The beginning of the week was for removing all the dead and rotting plants from the bed to prevent any diseases or fungus from growing in the soil. It would surely be needed again the following year to continue its bounty for the Fishers. Their bills were manageable but substantial. Mary had no qualms about helping again. After all, she had the hang of it and could learn from her mistakes. Next year's harvest would be even more profitable.

"Check the leaves first," Adel had instructed. "If you see evidence of insect eggs or larvae, be sure to throw it far away. You don't want your garden to be overrun with insects come springtime. However, if the leaves have no evidence of eggs, be sure to turn them back into the soil. They'll improve its tilth."

Mary carefully inspected all the leaves and had sorted them accordingly. After removing the dead plants, Mary had gone around the garden and pulled all invasive weeds out of the earth. They needed to be burned. *Perhaps Aaron will help dig a pit*, she pondered. With the invasives removed, the spring beds were readied. Mary sprinkled bone meal and manure across the beds before adding mulch to stop the weeds from overcoming the garden.

"Leave a thicker layer of mulch over the root vegetables," Adel had said. "It will help protect them from the frost and the snow."

Late in the week, Mary pruned the perennials. Adel had advised her to prune the herbs as well as the rhubarb and asparagus. As Mary carefully pruned the branches of a large, fragrant rosemary bush, she reflected on all the things that had happened in the fall. Despite her hesitation at the beginning of the season, autumn had been a time for endings and for beginnings.

First came her friendship with Adel, which could not have begun at a better time. It was an unlikely friendship that matured Mary. A mentor at such a vulnerable time in her life was precisely what she had needed. Adel allowed her—and showed her—how to prune away the deadwood parts of herself, to say goodbye to the garden—and the soul—she had known in the summer and spring and embrace the garden as it was in its current form. To appreciate their fruit, redirect their energies, and remove the unnecessary to have abundance. It was as though Adel's arrival presaged a greater change in Erie, for her appearance was followed by Isaiah's return. Then, everything returned to their rightful place. The harvest at the Fisher farm was one of the best crops in years. Rachel and Noah mended their relationship, much to Mary's relief. Isaiah's return had taken the pressure off Noah, and with the success of the harvest, Noah felt the weight of the financial burdens lifted. Then, there were Amos and Abigael who were making significant progress with their wedding plans, as were Sarah and Jacob. Everyone seemed to be in good spirits. Except for Aaron.

Aaron worried Mary. Ever since his father had returned, he seemed withdrawn and pensive. Though Rachel confided in Mary that, she, too, noticed that Aaron was not himself, she had been too preoccupied with Jo and Leora to inquire. Mary longed for some time with Aaron. He had been invited to help her winterize the garden. Thus far, he had not shown his face. Then, the garden gate creaked. Mary raised her head to smile. Aaron had come, complete with his familiar lopsided grin.

"Fancy meeting you here," Mary said.

"It's been a while," Aaron admitted.

Mary placed her garden shears on the ground and stood up, dusting off her skirt.

"How are the preparations going?"

"All right," Mary said. "I have finished preparing the beds, and I'm nearly done pruning all of the perennials. All that is left to do is dig a pit and burn the invasives. Wanna help?" She flashed him her cutest smile.

"I can help with that."

"The shovel's at the edge of the garden," Mary indicated.

Aaron nodded and fetched the shovel. He walked over to the south side and dug a hole. He worked quickly. While Aaron was preparing the burning pit, Mary finished pruning the rosemary, and then carefully collected the sprigs and placed them in her basket. She would make scented sachets as Christmas gifts. The rosemary fragrance would be a hit. Mary inspected Aaron's hole.

"This looks *gut*," Mary said.

"I'm glad you approve," Aaron said.

Mary blushed. She had not meant to sound condescending. *Aaron has a way...* though she never finished the thought.

"I'm just going to get some water in case we need it."

Mary nodded, left the man to his task, and set about collecting the bunches of invasives to place them at the edge of the pit.

"Watch out," Aaron said suddenly.

"What?"

"Your clothes," Aaron gestured.

Mary noticed that the skirt and the sleeves of her dress were covered in small, barbed burrs. "Oh no!" She quickly grabbed at them and threw them into the pit. Her beating heart nearly stopped when Aaron, with his strong, gentle touch, carefully removed the ones stuck on her wrists and forearms.

"There is something I've been wanting to tell you," Aaron said.

"What is it?" A man's presence is never needed in a girl's life until he is present. Then, she cannot imagine life without him. Mary had so missed Aaron in the garden because he could do what she could not: brute work with force and ferocity. A man is dangerous. Even a good man knows the harm he might inflict. What makes him good is his mastery over his strength for good. She, on the other hand, civilized him. He was weak for her, her smells, her grace. Mary walked about the garden doing her tasks with dainty elegance. Aaron had something to say. Mary was ready for him, ready for love, ready to explore courting her childhood friend.

"I'm leaving, Mary."

Mary was not ready for that. Her gasp revealed to them both that she had been holding her breath in anticipation. "You're leaving?"

Aaron nodded. "Now that my *daed* is well again, I've decided to take my *rumspringa*, like Sam."

This news surprised Mary. She had assumed that Aaron would stay to do his "running around" in the community like Rachel, Amos, and a hundred others. But Aaron in the city? Like Sam? He was a farm boy! Surely, he would die. "I did not realize that was something you wanted. I thought that you were happy here."

Aaron shrugged. "I'm not unhappy. I just feel stuck. Before my *daed* got sick, I didn't genuinely consider leaving for *rumspringa*. After this year, though, I think it would do me *gut* to experience some of the outside world. I love my family and the farm, but this year has aged me. I don't want to give up my youth just yet."

Mary understood precisely what Aaron meant. The year had been tough on all of them. They had all grown up. Perhaps that was how growing up worked; one moment you were a child, and the next, you were an adult.

"I think you've made the right decision," Mary heard herself say.

Aaron looked more relieved than surprised. "You get me, Mary. I knew you'd understand. You are one of my truest friends."

"And you, one of mine."

Aaron put his hand out to shake Mary's. Her throat swelled. She would greatly miss him.

"When are you leaving?" Mary asked.

"I'm not sure. Probably after Amos's wedding."

Mary nodded. That made sense. He would not want to miss his own brother's wedding. All the weddings were set to start that week, and they would last through early December, right before the weather turned for the worse.

"What will I do without you in the garden?" Mary asked.

"Look at this place." Aaron held out his hands as if to illustrate. "You don't need me, Mary."

Mary fought the urge to argue that she did need him, that she wanted him to stay, that she was ready for love. Aaron had been a true friend to Mary, especially in the garden. He had come whenever she'd needed him. Now, Mary needed to do the same in kind. His decision needed support, no matter how much she wished to the contrary. She prayed that she had not taken Aaron's presence in her life for granted. At the beginning of fall, Mary had been adamant that she would resolve how she felt about Aaron, and yet the events of the past few weeks had meant that she had forgotten her promise to herself, and now it had resolved itself. Aaron was leaving, and she regretted life moving on without her input. Would she ever figure out if they might have been more than just friends?

"Shall we start the fire?" Aaron asked.

That's what I had hoped you were going to do when you told me that you had something to say! Mary said to herself. She nodded and watched Aaron drop some dried leaves and twigs into the pit. He then added the pile of invasive plants and lit a match. Within seconds, the debris was burning. They both watched as the flames turned the leaves and sticks—the remnants of their adventure together—into ash. Loneliness had dug a pit in her stomach, hollowing out her emotions, leaving Mary destitute.

"Will you be back?" Mary asked abruptly. She hoped conversation would fill the void.

"I'll be back before you know it. You'll hardly notice I am gone."

"Then I won't say goodbye," Mary said.

"No," Aaron agreed. "No goodbyes, just see you later."

"See you later," Mary echoed.

❋ ❋ ❋

Mary and the young gardeners' story concludes in *Waiting for Winter Love* (Amish Love Through the Seasons Book 4). Join them on their winter adventure and find out how the story ends!
http://getbook.at/waitingforwinter

Thank you, readers!

Thank you for reading this book. It is important to me to share my stories with you and that you enjoy them. May I ask of you a favor? If you enjoyed this book, will you please take a moment to leave a review on Amazon and/or Goodreads? Thank you for your support!

Also, each week, I send my readers updates about my life as well as information about my new releases, freebies, promos, and book recommendations. If you're interested in receiving my weekly newsletter, please go to newsletter.sylviaprice.com, and it will ask you for your email. As a thank-you, you will receive a FREE exclusive short story that isn't available for purchase!

Blessings,
Sylvia

BOOKS IN THIS SERIES

Amish Love Through the Seasons
Featuring many of the beloved characters from Sylvia Price's bestseller, The Christmas Arrival, as well as a new cast of characters, Amish Love Through the Seasons centers around a group of teenagers as they find friendship, love, and hope in the midst of trials.

Tragedy strikes a small Amish community outside of Erie, Pennsylvania when Isaiah Fisher, a widower and father of three, is involved in a serious accident. When his family is left scrambling to pick up the pieces, the community unites to help the single father, but the hospital bills keep piling up. How will the family manage?

Mary Lapp, a youth in the community, decides to take up Isaiah's cause. She enlists the help of other teenagers to plant a garden and sell the produce. While tending to the garden, new relationships develop, but old ones are torn apart. With tensions mounting, will the youth get past their disagreements in order to reconcile and produce fruit? Will they each find love? Join them on their adventure through the seasons!

Seeds Of Spring Love (Book 1)

Sprouts Of Summer Love (Book 2)

Fruits Of Fall Love (Book 3)

Waiting For Winter Love (Book 4)

BOOKS BY THIS AUTHOR

The Christmas Arrival

Rachel Lapp is a young Amish woman who is the daughter of the community's bishop. She is in the midst of planning the annual Christmas Nativity play when newcomer Noah Miller arrives in town to spend Christmas with his cousins. Encouraged by her father to welcome the new arrival, Rachel asks Noah to be a part of the Nativity.

Despite Rachel's engagement to Samuel King, a local farmer, she finds herself irrevocably drawn to Noah and his carefree spirit. Reserved and slightly shy, Noah is hesitant to get involved in the play, but an unlikely friendship begins to develop between Rachel and Noah, bringing with it unexpected problems, including a seemingly harmless prank with life-threatening consequences that require a Christmas miracle.

Will Rachel honor her commitment to Samuel, or will Noah win her affections?

Join these characters on what is sure to be a heartwarming holiday adventure! Instead of waiting for each part to be released, enjoy the entire Christmas Arrival series in this exclusive collection!

Jonah's Redemption (Book 1)

Available for FREE on Amazon

Jonah has lost his community, and he's struggling to get by in the English world. He yearns for his Amish roots, but his past mistakes keep him from returning home.

Mary Lou is recovering from a medical scare. Her journey has impressed upon her how precious life is, so she decides to go on rumspringa to see the world.

While in the city, Mary Lou meets Jonah. Unable to understand his foul attitude, especially towards her, she makes every effort to share her faith with him. As she helps him heal from his past, an attraction develops.

Will Jonah's heart soften towards Mary Lou? What will God do with these two broken people?

Jonah's Redemption Boxed Set (Books 2-5, Epilogue, And Companion Story)

If you loved Jonah's Redemption: Book 1 (available for free on Amazon), grab the rest of the series in this special boxed set featuring Books 2-5, plus a bonus epilogue and companion story, "Jonah's Reminiscence."

Mary Lou's fiancé leaves her as soon as tragedy strikes. Unwilling to resent him, she chooses, instead, to find him. Her misfortunes pile up in her quest to return Jonah to the Amish faith, but she is undeterred, for God has given her a mission.

Will Mary Lou's faith be enough to help them get through the countless obstacles that are thrown their way? Do Jonah and Mary Lou have a chance at happiness?

Join Jonah and Mary Lou as they wrestle with love, a life worth living, and their unique faith in Christ. Enjoy the conclusion of Jonah's Redemption in this exclusive boxed set, with a bonus epilogue and companion story!

Songbird Cottage Beginnings (Pleasant Bay Prequel)

Available for FREE on Amazon

Set on Canada's picturesque Cape Breton Island, this book is perfect for those who enjoy new beginnings and countryside landscapes.

Sam MacAuley and his wife Annalize are total opposites. When Sam wants to leave city life in Halifax to get a plot of land on Cape Breton Island, where he grew up, his wife wants nothing to do with his plans and opts to move herself and their three boys back to her home country of South Africa.

As Sam settles into a new life on his own, his friend Lachlan encourages him to get back into the dating scene. Although he meets plenty of women, he longs to find the one with whom he wants to share the rest of his life. Will Sam ever meet "the one"?

Get to know Sam and discover the origins of the Songbird Cottage.

This is the prequel to the rest of the Pleasant Bay series.

The Songbird Cottage Boxed Set (Pleasant Bay Complete Series Collection)

If you loved Songbird Cottage Beginnings (available for free on Amazon), grab the rest of the series in this special boxed set.

Amazon bestselling author Sylvia Price's Pleasant Bay series is a feel-good read about family loyalties and second chances set on Canada's picturesque Cape Breton Island. This series is perfect for those who enjoy sweet romances and countryside landscapes. Enjoy all these sweet romance books in one collection for the first time!

Emma Copeland and her daughters, Claire and Isabelle, spend their summers at Songbird Cottage in Pleasant Bay, Nova Scotia. While there, Emma enjoys the company of her ruggedly handsome neighbor, Sam MacAuley, but when something happens between them, she vows never to return to Songbird Cottage.

When Emma turns fifty, she rushes into a marriage with smooth-talking Andrew Schönfeld, but when he suddenly dies, Emma loses everything.

With her life in shambles, and with nowhere else to stay, Emma returns to Songbird Cottage. Despite leaving without an explanation eighteen years ago, Sam is quick to Emma's aid when she arrives on Cape Breton.

As the beauty and peacefulness of Pleasant Bay begin to heal Emma, she gets some shocking news, and she discovers that she's unwelcomed at Songbird Cottage. Will she be able to piece her life back together and get another chance at happiness?

Join Emma Copeland and her daughters, Claire and Isabelle, get to know their family and neighbors, and explore the magic of Songbird Cottage.

Included in this set are all the popular titles:

The Songbird Cottage
Return to Songbird Cottage

Escape to Songbird Cottage
Secrets of Songbird Cottage
Seasons at Songbird Cottage

ABOUT THE AUTHOR

Now an Amazon bestselling author, Sylvia Price is an author of Amish and contemporary romance and women's fiction. She especially loves writing uplifting stories about second chances!

Sylvia was inspired to write about the Amish as a result of the enduring legacy of Mennonite missionaries in her life. While living with them for three weeks, they got her a library card and encouraged her to start reading to cope with the loss of television and radio, giving Sylvia a new-found appreciation for books.

Although raised in the cosmopolitan city of Montréal, Sylvia spent her adolescent and young adult years in Nova Scotia, and the beautiful countryside landscapes and ocean views serve as the backdrop to her contemporary novels.

After meeting and falling in love with an American while living abroad, Sylvia now resides in the US. She spends her days writing, hoping to inspire the next generation to read more stories. When she's not writing, Sylvia stays busy making sure her three young children are alive and well-fed.

Subscribe to Sylvia's newsletter at newsletter.sylviaprice.com to stay in the loop about new releases, freebies, promos, and more. As a thank-you, you will receive a FREE exclusive short story that isn't available for purchase!

Learn more about Sylvia at amazon.com/author/sylviaprice and goodreads.com/author/show/1134593.Sylvia_Price.

Follow Sylvia on Facebook at facebook.com/sylviapriceauthor for updates.

Join Sylvia's Advanced Reader Copies (ARC) team at arcteam.sylviaprice.com to get her books for free before they are released in exchange for honest reviews.

www.ingramcontent.com/pod-product-compliance
Lightning Source LLC
LaVergne TN
LVHW092146230125
802046LV00032B/637